JANICE MAYNARD

—

HIS HEIR, HER SECRET

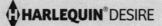

HARLEQUIN® DESIRE

If you purchased this book without a cover you should be aware
that this book is stolen property. It was reported as "unsold and
destroyed" to the publisher, and neither the author nor the
publisher has received any payment for this "stripped book."

Recycling programs
for this product may
not exist in your area.

ISBN-13: 978-1-335-97155-5

His Heir, Her Secret

Copyright © 2018 by Janice Maynard

All rights reserved. Except for use in any review, the reproduction or
utilization of this work in whole or in part in any form by any electronic,
mechanical or other means, now known or hereafter invented, including
xerography, photocopying and recording, or in any information storage
or retrieval system, is forbidden without the written permission of the
publisher, Harlequin Enterprises Limited, 22 Adelaide St. West, 40th Floor,
Toronto, ON M5H 4E3, Canada.

This is a work of fiction. Names, characters, places and incidents are
either the product of the author's imagination or are used fictitiously,
and any resemblance to actual persons, living or dead, business
establishments, events or locales is entirely coincidental.

This edition published by arrangement with Harlequin Books S.A.

For questions and comments about the quality of this book,
please contact us at CustomerService@Harlequin.com.

® and TM are trademarks of Harlequin Enterprises Limited or its
corporate affiliates. Trademarks indicated with ® are registered in the
United States Patent and Trademark Office, the Canadian Intellectual
Property Office and in other countries.

Printed in U.S.A.

www.Harlequin.com

"Seriously, Brody. You owe me nothing, nothing at all."

"You're carrying my baby." His gaze was stormy.

"But you don't really want to be a father, do you? Be honest. You don't even want to be a husband. Why would we put ourselves through a sham that will only lead to heartbreak?"

His brooding stare made her nipples tighten against the slippery fabric of her bra. She had never met a man as unflinchingly masculine as Brody Stewart. It was easy to imagine him in another time, a fiery chieftain leading his clan.

"Would marrying me be such a terrible fate?"

In his deep blue eyes, she saw a hint of the same turmoil she had carried with her every day since the baby became a reality. The prospect of being Brody Stewart's bride was a fantasy she had entertained briefly back in the fall. The intensity of their combustible attraction had raised the possibility that Brody might be *the one*.

Even now it would be far too easy to fall prey to the fairy tale. But she had done that once before and been burned. She was older...wiser.

* * *

His Heir, Her Secret is part of the Highland Heroes duet from *USA TODAY* bestselling author Janice Maynard!

Dear Reader,

Several years ago my husband and I took a trip to the Scottish Highlands. We fell in love with the castles and the moors and the way the light falls across the mountains. It was magic.

When I began planning my next duet for Harlequin Desire, I immediately imagined a pair of Scottish brothers who somehow ended up in the United States. The ideas took off from there.

I had such fun writing Brody and Cate's romance. Neither of them thought the other was anything more than a crazy two-week affair. But life has a way of taking twists and turns.

I hope you enjoy this story, and I hope you'll look for next month's follow-up book when Duncan Stewart, Brody's younger brother, finds his own happily-ever-after.

Happy summer, and happy reading!

Janice Maynard

USA TODAY bestselling author **Janice Maynard** loved books and writing even as a child. But it took multiple rejections before she sold her first manuscript. Since 2002, she has written over forty-five books and novellas. Janice lives in east Tennessee with her husband, Charles. They love hiking, traveling and spending time with family.

You can connect with Janice at janicemaynard.com, Twitter.com/janicemaynard, Facebook.com/janicemaynardreaderpage and Instagram.com/janicemaynard.

Books by Janice Maynard

Harlequin Desire

The Kavanaghs of Silver Glen

A Not-So-Innocent Seduction
Baby for Keeps
Christmas in the Billionaire's Bed
Twins on the Way
Second Chance with the Billionaire
How to Sleep with the Boss
For Baby's Sake

Highland Heroes

His Heir, Her Secret

Visit her Author Profile page at Harlequin.com, or janicemaynard.com, for more titles.

For all of my friends who have ever fantasized about owning a quaint bookstore in a charming small town...this one's for you... 😊

One

The Scotsman was back. Heart pounding, hands sweating, Cate Everett leaned over her old-fashioned, nicked-up porcelain sink and eased the curtain aside with one finger. From the vantage point of her upstairs apartment, she had a perfect view of the comings and goings across the street.

Brody Stewart. The man she hadn't seen in four months and believed she would never see again. Brody Stewart. Six feet and more of broad shoulders, sinewy muscles and a rough-velvet brogue of a voice that could shuck the panties off a girl before she knew what was happening. The Scotsman was back.

She wasn't ready. Dear Lord, she wasn't ready.

Her freshly brewed cup of tea sat cooling on the table behind her. The late February day had been icy and drear, a perfect match for the mood that had plagued her since climbing out of bed at dawn. She'd thought the comforting drink would cheer her up.

Instead, a clatter of slamming doors and deep male voices had distracted her...driven her to the window. And now she knew. The Scotsman was back.

In all fairness, Cate had never seen disaster coming four months ago. When a man's grandmother introduces you to her grandson, a woman usually thinks the guy can't get his own dates.

Only in this case, it wasn't true. Brody Stewart could have any woman he wanted with one twinkle of his long-lashed, indigo-blue eyes. She still remembered the tiny lines that crinkled at the corners of those gorgeous eyes when he smiled. Brody smiled a lot.

Oh, jeez. Her legs wobbled in sync with the drunken butterflies in her stomach. She needed to sit down. She needed to drink her tea. But she couldn't tear herself away from the window.

On the street below, a tiny, gray-haired lady gave orders to two remarkably similar men. Brody was one. The other must be Duncan, his younger brother. Suitcases came out of the trunk of a rental car. Hugs were exchanged. Snowflakes danced on the breeze.

None of the three people she spied on seemed to notice the cold. Perhaps because they hailed from the Scottish Highlands...a place where winter winds scoured the moors, and bloodlines went as far back as the hearty stock of warring clans and beyond.

Cate wiped damp palms on her faded jeans. She

needed to focus. Voyeurism and dithering weren't going to accomplish a thing. Besides, she had a shop to run.

Forcing herself to step back and abandon her intense fascination with the tableau on the street, she cradled her teacup in two trembling hands, drank most of the cold liquid and set the delicate china aside before making her way downstairs. Lunch break, such as it was, was over.

For five years she had found solace and pride in her charmingly eccentric bookshop, Dog-Eared Pages. The little store with the uneven hardwood floors and the rows of antique bookshelves held a place of honor on the main street of Candlewick, North Carolina. From the spring solstice until almost Thanksgiving, tourists came and went, bringing dollars and life to the region.

Tucked away in the Blue Ridge Mountains an hour from Asheville, Candlewick hearkened back to a simpler time. Neighbors knew each other's business, crime was rare and the quality of life made up for the lack of first-run movie theaters and big-name restaurants.

Cate straightened the local History section and dusted one volume at a time, congratulating herself on avoiding the front of the store. She didn't need to know what was happening across the street. It had nothing to do with her.

Without warning, the tinkling of a bell above the door announced the arrival of a customer. Cate's heart stopped for a full three seconds, and then lurched ahead with a sickening whoosh when she recognized her visitor.

She cleared her dry throat. "Miss Izzy. What can I do for you?"

Isobel Stewart stood barely five feet tall but carried herself with the personality of an Amazon. Decades ago she had left her parents' home in Inverness for a secretarial job in the big city of Edinburgh. While there, she met a charismatic American who had come to Scotland for a study-abroad semester.

After a whirlwind courtship, Isobel married the lad and followed him back to the United States— Candlewick, North Carolina, to be precise. She embraced her new life with only one request, that she keep her maiden name. Her new husband not only agreed, but also legally changed his last name to hers so that the Stewart line would continue. Together, the young couple launched a business building cabins in the mountains.

The intervening years produced vast wealth and a single son. Unfortunately for his parents, the young man felt the pull of his Scottish roots and after college settled in the Highlands. *His* two sons were the two men Cate had been spying on across the street. Izzy's grandsons.

Isobel Stewart scanned the titles on the New Release shelf. "I want ye to come to dinner tonight, Cate. Brody is back. And he's brought Duncan with him this time."

"You must be thrilled," Cate said, avoiding the question. Actually, it was more of a command. Isobel rarely accepted no for an answer.

The little woman suddenly looked every one of her ninety-two years. "I need you," she muttered as if mortified by her weakness.

The smell of lemon polish permeated the air. Cate leaned a hip against the oak counter that supported the cash register. "What's wrong, Miss Izzy?"

When the old Scottish lady blinked back tears, Cate couldn't tell if they were genuine or manipulative.

Isobel's bottom lip quivered. "I don't have room in the apartment for *two* huge men, so I've told the lads they have to stay up at the big house."

The *big house* was Isobel's lavish and incredibly beautiful property on the mountaintop above Candlewick. Izzy hadn't been able to spend the night there since her husband died six months before. Like many of the businesses in Candlewick, Stewart Properties was housed in a historic building on Main Street. Izzy had taken to sleeping on the second floor above her office.

"Makes sense," Cate said carefully, sensing a trap. "But what does that have to do with me?"

"The boys wanted to surprise me for my birthday. They've hired a caterer to prepare dinner for us tonight. I hadn't the heart to tell them I didn't want to come."

"Oh, I didn't remember it was today. Happy birthday. But Brody was here before. Surely the two of you spent time up on the mountain."

"He did a few chores for me. Checked on things. I pretended like I was busy. And since it was just Brody, he slept on the sofa, ye know…in the apartment…with me."

"Miss Izzy…" Cate trailed off, searching for words. "Your grandsons must have an inkling of how you feel. Maybe this is their way of breaking the ice. It's been six months. The longer you stay away, the more difficult it will be. I'm guessing they planned the birthday dinner to lure you up there."

"It doesn't feel like months," the old woman said, her words wistful. "It seems like yesterday. My dear Geoffrey's spirit is a ghost in every room of that house. Go with me," Izzy pleaded. Gnarled, arthritic hands twisted at her waist. For a split second, Cate witnessed the depth of Isobel Stewart's anguish at losing the love of her life.

"It's a family celebration," Cate said. "It will seem odd if I come."

"Not at all," Izzy said. "It was actually Brody's idea."

Five hours later Cate found herself on the doorstep of Stewart Properties, bouncing from one foot to the other in a futile attempt to keep warm. At the curb, she had left the engine running in her modest four-door sedan.

At last, when Cate's fingers were numb, Izzy appeared. She looked remarkably chipper for someone who was about to face an unpleasant experience. "Right on time," Izzy said. "You're a lovely young lass. Men don't like a woman who can't be punctual."

Cate helped the old woman into the car. Izzy was wrapped from head to toe in a brown wool coat and a heavy woven scarf in brown and beige. "That's a stereotype, Miss Izzy. I'm sure there are as many men as women who have trouble being on time."

Isobel snorted and changed the subject. "I thought ye'd wear a dress," she complained.

Cate extracted the car from the tight parking space and adjusted the defroster. "It's going to be close to twenty degrees tonight. These are my best dress pants." She'd worn them back when she was on her way to becoming a doctor…in the days before her world fell apart.

"Pants, schmantz. Brody and Duncan are hot-blooded men. I'm sure they would have enjoyed seeing a glimpse of leg. Yours are spectacular, bonnie young Cate. When you're my age, you'll wish ye'd appreciated what ye had when you had it."

There was no arguing with the antiquated, sexually regressive logic of a woman in her nineties.

Cate sighed. Unfortunately, the road up the mountain was easily traversed and not long at all. When they pulled up in front of the Stewart mansion—Cate would be hard-pressed to describe it as anything else—they had time to spare. Izzy's home was spectacular. Weathered mountain stone, rough-hewn lumber, copper guttering, giant multipaned windows that brought the outdoors inside... This magnificent architectural gem had once graced the cover of *Southern Living*.

Cate touched the petite woman's arm. "Are you going to be okay?"

Izzy sniffed. "Outliving your friends and contemporaries is bollocks, Cate."

"Miss Izzy!" Her friend's lack of respect for social convention still caught her off guard at times.

"Don't be prissy. What's the point of getting old if ye can't say what ye please?"

"So back to my original question. Are you going to be okay?"

Izzy gazed through the windshield, her cheeks damp. "He built that house as a thank-you to me. Did you know that?"

"No, ma'am, I didn't. A thank-you for what?"

"Giving up Scotland. My family. My home. Coming here to America with him. Silly fool." She stopped. Her throat worked. "I'd have given all that and more for one more day with the auld codger."

Cate felt her own throat tighten, and not only because of Izzy's emotional return to the house where she had spent a decades-long marriage. Izzy had pledged herself and her heart to a man who was her soul mate. Cate had never even come close. And now she had made the most wretched mistake of her life.

She turned off the engine and gripped the steering wheel. Brody was inside that house. What was she going to say to him?

Izzy moved restively. "Might as well get it over with," she muttered. "I'll not cry, mind you. Too many tears shed already. Besides, I don't want the lads to think they've done wrong by me. Let's go, Cate, my girl."

The two women scuttled up the flagstone walkway, buffeted by an icy wind. Moments later the double, burnished-oak front doors swung open wide. The massive chandelier in the foyer spilled light into the darkness. The diminutive Scotswoman was caught up in the enthusiastic hugs of her two über-masculine grandsons.

Brody's thick, wavy chestnut hair shone with strands of reddish-gold mixed in. Duncan's was a darker brown and straighter. He had the rich brown eyes to match. Though the brothers were alike in many ways, Izzy had once upon a time explained to Cate that Brody favored his Irish-born mother while Duncan was a younger version of his Grandda.

Now that Cate had finally met Duncan, she agreed. It was astonishing to see how much Brody's younger brother resembled Geoffrey Stewart. She wondered if it was painful for Izzy to look at Duncan and see the memory of her young husband in the flesh.

Cate hung back, still not sure why she had come. Izzy seemed to be handling things with grace and bravery. It was Cate whose stomach quivered with nerves.

Izzy drew Cate forward. "Cate, my dear, meet Duncan."

Duncan Stewart lifted her hand and kissed the back of it. "Charmed, Miss Everett."

Brody snorted. "Knock it off, Duncan."

Duncan held up his hands, visibly protesting his innocence. "What? What did I do?"

"Go check on the caterer, would you?"

Moments later Duncan bore his grandmother deeper into the house, leaving Cate alone with Brody.

The man who had avoided eyeing her until now, gave her a crooked grin. "Surprise, lass. I'm back."

Brody wasn't an idiot. He knew when a woman was glad to see him and when she wasn't. Cate Everett looked like someone who had swallowed bad milk. His pride took a hit, but he maintained his smile with effort. "It was nice of you to come with Granny. I know she's been dreading this moment."

Cate took off her coat slowly and handed it to him. "Then why force the issue?"

He shrugged, turning to hang up Cate's wrap. "There are decisions to be made. My ninety-two-year-old grandmother has been sleeping in a closet-sized room with the barest of essentials. Grandda is gone. This house is still here. We can't pretend anymore."

Cate's jaw tightened. "Are you always so sure you know what's best for everyone?"

He cocked his head, studying her from a distance, even though he thought about grabbing her up and kissing her soundly. The last time the two of them had seen each other, they had been naked and breathless in Cate's bed.

"Have I upset ye in some way, Cate? I had to leave. You knew that."

A month after his grandfather's funeral, Brody had returned to Candlewick to spend time with his grandmother and to assess the state of the family business. Stewart Properties was a thriving company with a stellar reputation in the United States.

Unfortunately, Geoffrey Stewart was gone now. Brody's own father had no desire to return to the States permanently. So something had to be done about Granny Isobel.

Brody had spent four weeks in North Carolina, two of them wildly in lust with the beautiful and brilliant Cate Everett. By day he had been a dutiful grandson. At night he had found himself drawn time and again to the woman who had a reputation around the small town for being kind but standoffish. With Brody, she had been anything but...

To be honest, the depth of his physical infatuation had made him the tiniest bit uncomfortable. He understood the mechanics of sexual attraction. He'd even had his share of serious relationships. But when his grandmother introduced him to her friend and neighbor, Cate Everett, Brody had felt like a tongue-tied adolescent.

Cate was a mix of femme fatale and spinster school-teacher. Her pale blond hair was like sunshine on a winter afternoon, though she kept it tucked up in a tight knot on the back of her head most days, the kind of knot that looked headache-producing from the get-go.

But when she let it down…hot damn. Even now Brody's fingers itched to touch the fall of silk that had spilled across his chest and still featured in his fantasies.

She was tall, five-ten at least. Brody knew the curves and valleys of her alluring shape, but Cate kept her body mostly hidden beneath loose cardigans and below-the-knee jumpers. He had no clue why a woman as intensely feminine as she was would make a concerted effort to hide in plain sight.

After a long, awkward silence, she cast him a sideways glance, her small smile rueful. "I'm sorry. It's been a long day. It's nice to see you again, Brody."

He wrinkled his nose. "Nice?"

"I didn't want to give you any ideas."

"About what?"

"You *know* what," Cate said crossly. "I'm not interested in picking up where we left off."

"Maybe I wasn't going to ask." He taunted her deliberately. Her prickly attitude was both frustrating and a challenge. He'd never met a woman with as many complicated layers as Cate Everett.

Cate sighed. "It's cold here in the foyer. Do you mind if we go find the others? I'm starving."

"Of course. I do remember how ye like to eat."

When Cate flushed to her hairline, he smiled inwardly. On one memorable occasion last fall, the two of them had climbed out of Cate's bed at midnight and fixed scrambled eggs and bacon, because they had skipped dinner in favor of urgent, mind-blowing sex.

Cate knew her way around Isobel's house, so he let her lead. She and Granny had been friends for several years. Although Brody had pumped his grandmother for information about the aloof American, she had fed him few details.

They found Duncan and Isobel in the dining room. The caterer who was preparing dinner had set an elegant table with Stewart china and silver and crystal. Brody's grandmother stood behind the chair that had been her husband's and rested her hands on the tall back. "One of you boys should sit here," she said with the tiniest quaver in her voice.

Brody and Duncan looked at each other. Cate winced. Finally, Brody shook his head. "I can't, Granny. Neither can Duncan."

"Then why did ye make me come up here?" she snapped, her eyes welling with tears. "If my own grandsons won't move on, how am I supposed to?"

Two

To Brody's relief, Cate stepped forward. "What if I take Mr. Geoffrey's chair tonight, Miss Izzy? It would be my honor. You can sit here beside me."

Brody mouthed a *thank-you* to her over his grandmother's head. Izzy had some definite ideas about how the future was going to play out, and she wasn't above emotional manipulation to get her way. He and Duncan had spent hours discussing possibilities, but no single solution had presented itself as of yet.

Without extra leaves in the antique table, the four adults sat in an intimate enclave, Cate and Duncan at the head and foot, Brody and Izzy to Cate's left and right. Fortunately, the caterer was on his game, and the elaborate meal kicked off immediately, helping ease the moments of tension. The brothers had ordered all of Izzy's favorites: fresh brook trout, seasoned carrots and potatoes, flaky biscuits and tender asparagus, all washed down with an expensive zinfandel. Though the elderly woman's capacity for food was modest, she ate with delight, her worn, wrinkled face aglow.

Cate did her part, not only by sitting in for the ghost at the table, but also by contributing with her quick wit and stimulating conversation. The four adults covered books and politics and international affairs.

Duncan, much to Brody's dismay, seemed especially taken with Cate. That was a really bad idea. Maybe Brody should have given his little brother a heads-up that the lady was spoken for.

He choked on a bit of carrot and had to wash it down with half a glass of water, red-faced and stunned. If Duncan ended up being the one to move here with Granny and keep the business afloat, it made perfect sense that he and Cate might hit it off.

Apparently, Brody did a poor job of disguising his emotions. Granny Isobel waved a fork at him. "Ye okay there, my lad? Did you find a bone in your fish?"

Brody grimaced. "I'm fine."

Cate gazed at him curiously with catlike green eyes that always made him uncomfortable. He didn't particularly want a woman peering into his soul. Surely it was his imagination that suggested she could read his every thought.

Desperate to deflect the attention from himself, he nudged his brother's foot under the table. "Duncan here has some good ideas about the company, Granny."

Isobel perked up. "I'm listening."

Duncan glared at his brother with a fierceness that promised retribution. He cleared his throat. "The thing is, Granny, I think it makes a lot of sense to put Stewart Properties on the market. The American economy has rebounded. It's an optimal time to sell. Ye shouldn't be living alone at your age anyway, and just think how happy Dad would be if you moved back to Scotland."

Everything in the room went silent. The four adults sat frozen in an uncomfortable tableau. The caterer was nowhere to be seen, undoubtedly in the kitchen whipping up a fabulous dessert.

Cate cleared her throat and stood. "This is family business," she said quietly. "If you'll excuse me, I'll go to the library and amuse myself."

Before Brody could protest, Isobel lifted her chin and stared them down with the arrogance of a queen. "Ye're not leaving, Cate. I asked you to come with me tonight, and I consider ye one of my dearest friends. It appears I may need someone on my side."

Brody frowned. "That's not fair, Granny, and you know it. Duncan and I love you dearly and want the best for everyone involved. There are no *sides* in this conversation."

His grandmother huffed, a sound he recognized from his childhood and all the years in between. "When I'm dead, ye can do whatever you like with your inheritance. For now, though, this company Geoffrey and I built with our sweat and tears is all I have left of him. To be honest, I'm glad you forced the issue of me coming back to the house. I didn't realize how much I had missed it."

"We could keep the house," Brody said. He had thrown his brother under the bus. Now it was time for Brody to take some of the heat.

Isobel glared at him. "What part of *not selling* didn't you understand? I'm old. Don't you get it? I won't be here much longer. Besides, I have two excellent managers who are working out very well in Geoffrey's absence."

Cate brought in reinforcements, giving Brody a look of sympathy. "But remember, Miss Izzy, Herman is getting ready to move to California…to be near his ailing parents, and it's too huge an operation for Kevin to manage all on his own. You said so yourself."

Instead of being cowed, Isobel seemed energized by the conflict. "Then one of these two will pick up the slack. Surely that's not too much for an old woman to ask of her grandsons."

Again, silence descended, heavy with the weight of familial expectations. Cate tried to help, God bless her generous soul. "Brody has his boat business in Skye, Miss Izzy. Surely you wouldn't ask him to give that up. And Duncan is a partner in that, right?" She lifted an eyebrow.

Duncan nodded. "I am. Brody still owns the controlling share, but I handle all the financial operations."

Izzy wasn't impressed. "So sell *your* business. You can both move here. Stewart Properties is going to belong to you both one day anyway. Your father doesn't need anything of mine."

Isobel's son, Brody and Duncan's father, was a world-famous artist with galleries all over the British Isles. He was wildly successful and obscenely wealthy. Even so, he had insisted his boys get good educations and find their own paths in life. Brody appreciated his father's contribution to the launch of the boating business, but that financial obligation had been repaid long ago.

Brody ran a hand through his hair. Never in his wildest dreams had he imagined his grandmother was going to be such a handful. Whatever happened to sweet, docile old women who knitted and crocheted and went to church on Sundays and let the menfolk take care of them?

"Maybe we should all sleep on this, Granny. Duncan and I are jet-lagged anyway. I vote we enjoy the rest of dinner."

The caterer entered the dining room bearing a tray of warm apple tarts drizzled with fresh cream. The interruption was timely as far as Brody was concerned. The only reason he and Duncan had been dispatched to North Carolina was to settle their grandmother's business affairs and bring her home to Scotland.

The chances of that happening were becoming more remote by the minute.

Unpleasant subjects were abandoned over coffee and dessert. Brody allowed himself, for the first time that evening, to truly study Cate. He had hoped his four-month-old recollections of her were exaggerated. Surely her skin wasn't as soft as he remembered…or her voice as husky.

When she laughed at something Duncan said, Brody actually felt a pain in his chest. She was everything he had dreamed about and infinitely better in person. Which only made his dilemma all the more complicated. He sure as hell couldn't play fast and loose with a woman his grandmother held in high regard.

Not that it mattered. For some reason Cate had changed. Four months ago she had smiled at him as if she meant it. Now her gaze slid away from his time and again. Even if he wanted her in his bed again—or hers—it seemed unlikely that Cate was on the same page.

By nine o'clock, Isobel was visibly drooping.

Cate noticed, too. She touched the elderly woman on the hand. "I think it's my bedtime, Miss Izzy. Are you ready to head down the mountain?"

"Soon," Isobel said. "But since these boys forced my hand, and I'm here, I'd like to walk through the house before I go. Duncan, you come with me. Brody, entertain Cate until I get back."

When the other two walked out of the room, Brody chuckled. "I swear she doesn't weigh a hundred pounds soaking wet, but she's got all of us at the end of a tight leash."

Cate nodded. "I don't envy you and Duncan. Changing her mind won't be easy."

"And it might be impossible. Which means removing her by force or finding a way to maintain the status quo until it's her time to go."

Cate picked up a silver chalice on the mahogany sideboard and studied it intently. "Have you given any thought to relocating for a few years? For her?"

Brody sensed a trap in the question, but he couldn't pin it down. "My life is in Scotland," he said flatly. "I've spent seven years building my boat business. I need the water. It speaks to me. Nothing here compares."

"I see."

He walked around the table that separated them and touched her hair. "I'll ask again, Cate. Have I done something to upset you?" He wasn't adept at playing games, and he would have sworn that Cate was not the kind of woman to give a man fits.

"Of course not," she said, though her tone belied the words.

He took her wrist in a gentle grasp and turned her to face him. "I've missed ye, Cate." Yearning slammed into him with the punch of a sledgehammer. His hands trembled with the need to drag her close and kiss her.

His head lowered. She looked up at him, big-eyed, her gaze a conundrum he couldn't understand. "I missed you, too," she whispered.

And then it happened. Maybe he moved. Maybe she did. Suddenly, his mouth was on hers and she was kissing him back. Their lips clung together and separated and mated again. She tasted like apples and pure heaven. His heart pounded. His sex hardened. For a single blinding moment of clarity, he knew this was one of the reasons he had come back to North Carolina. "Cate," he muttered.

The caterer returned to clear the table, and Cate jerked away, her expression caught somewhere between horror and what appeared to be revulsion…which made no sense at all. They had been good together. Sensational.

Cate swept the back of her hand across her mouth

and whispered urgently, "You have lip gloss on your chin."

He picked up a napkin, wiped his face and looked at the pink stain on the white linen. Before he could say anything, Duncan and Isobel walked into the room.

Brody's grandmother had been crying...her eyes were red-rimmed. But she seemed calm and at peace. Brody shot his brother a quick glance. Duncan grimaced but nodded. Apparently, all was well.

"We'll go now," Cate said.

Isobel followed her through the house and into the front foyer. While Duncan helped the women with their coats, Brody brooded. "I'll drive you down the mountain," he said. "It's dark, and it's late."

Cate frowned. "Don't be ridiculous. I'm perfectly capable of negotiating this mountain. Unlike you, I like it here."

Brody winced inwardly. He hadn't been wrong. *Something* was going on with Cate. He lowered his voice. "Will ye walk Granny upstairs and make sure she's settled?"

"Of course." Cate pulled away from him and put on her gloves. "I've been looking after Miss Izzy for a long time. You people came over for the funeral and left again. She's important to me. I won't let her down."

"The implication being that I'm a disappointment."

Cate shrugged and lifted her hair from beneath her collar. "If the shoe fits."

Duncan intervened. "If the two of you can quit squabbling, I think Granny's ready for bed."

Isobel spoke up. "I can wait. At my age, I don't need

as much sleep. Besides, watching Brody try to woo Cate is a hoot and a half."

"There's no wooing," Cate protested, her cheeks turning red. "We were merely having a difference of opinion. Cultural differences and all that."

Now Brody felt his own face flush. "I'm Scottish, not an alien species."

She sniffed audibly. "It doesn't really matter, does it? Miss Izzy is a North Carolinian, and so am I. You and Duncan are merely passing through."

With that pointed remark, Cate ushered Isobel out into the cold and slammed the door behind them.

Duncan whistled long and loud. "What in the hell did you do to piss her off? We haven't even been in Candlewick twenty-four hours."

"I don't know what you're talking about," Brody lied.

"I may be a wee bit younger than you are, but I've tangled with my share of fiery lasses. The sexual tension between you and the lovely Cate is nuclear."

"Don't call her *lovely*," Brody snapped. "Don't call her anything."

Duncan rocked back on his heels and wrapped his arms across his chest. "Damn. You're a fast worker, bro, but even *you* aren't that good. Something happened four months ago, didn't it?"

"None of your business."

"You messed around with that gorgeous woman and then went home. Cold, Brody. Really cold. No wonder she looks as if she wants to strangle you."

"It wasn't like that. Granny introduced us. Cate and I became…close."

"For the entire four weeks?"

"The last two. It wasn't anything either of us planned. Can we talk about something else please?"

"Okay. What are we going to do about Granny?"

Hell. This topic was not much better. "We have to convince her to sell. She's too damned old to be here on her own."

"She has Cate."

"Cate's not family."

"I don't think Granny cares. That old woman crossed an ocean with a brand-new husband and started a brand-new life. She's tough. Losing Grandda was a huge blow, but she's still upright and fighting. What if we make her go home to Scotland, and it's the final blow? She hasn't lived there since she was a very young woman. Candlewick and the business and this house are all she knows."

"Aren't you forgetting our father, her *son*?"

"Dad is an eccentric. He and Granny love each other, but it works really well long distance. That's not a reason to kidnap her. She's an independent soul. I don't want to break her spirit."

"And you think I do?" Brody's frustration spilled over in a shout. "Sorry," he muttered.

Duncan locked the front door and turned off the lights. "We're both beat. Let's call it a night. Maybe we'll have a flash of inspiration tomorrow."

"I doubt it."

Brody fell asleep instantly, but surfaced four hours later, completely disoriented and wide-awake. After a few seconds the fog cleared. It was midmorning back home. On a good day he'd be out on the loch with the wind in his hair and the sun on his back. He slung an arm across his face and told himself not to panic. No one could *make* him move to America. That was ludicrous.

Without warning, an image of Cate Everett filled his brain. He would never admit it, but even with an ocean between them, Cate had been on his mind most days over the past four months. There was something about her gentle smile and husky laughter and the way her hair spilled like warm silk across his chest when they were in bed together.

She wasn't exactly uninhibited between the sheets. In fact, the first three times they had been intimate, she'd insisted on having the lights off. He'd thought her shyness was charming and sweet. He'd considered it a personal triumph when she'd actually let him strip her naked in broad daylight and make her scream his name.

The memory dampened his forehead and caused his jaw to clench. The house was plenty cool, but suddenly the bed felt like a prison.

Bloody hell. He pulled on a clean pair of boxers and wandered barefoot through the silent hallways to the kitchen. The generous space had been renovated a decade ago. Despite Isobel's advanced age, she had never fit the stereotype of a little old lady. She embraced change and even loved technology. Stewart Properties was a sophisticated, cutting-edge company with an incredibly healthy bottom line.

He poured himself a glass of orange juice and downed it in three swallows. Brody owed his grandmother a great deal. She had helped him through a very painful period of his life when his parents divorced. He'd been fifteen and totally oblivious to the undercurrents in the house.

When the end came, life had become unbearable. Isobel insisted that her two boys come to North Carolina for a long visit, long enough for the worst of the trauma to ease. These mountains had provided healing.

Under the circumstances, Brody had a very serious debt to pay.

Even knowing that, his gut churned. Staying in Candlewick would mean dealing with Cate and his muddled feelings.

It was far easier to live on another continent.

After half an hour of pacing, his feet were icy, and sleep was out of the question. Without second-guessing himself, he returned to his bedroom and dressed rapidly. Duncan wouldn't need transportation at this hour.

Brody guided the boring rental car down the winding mountain road, careful to stay on the correct side of the road. It helped that no one else was out at this hour. Soon he reached the outskirts of town. Candlewick still slept. Main Street was deserted.

He parked the car and filched a small handful of pea gravel from the nicely landscaped flower beds at the bank. Then he eyed Cate's bookstore with a frown. The striped burgundy and green awning that covered the front of the shop was going to make this difficult.

Though he had sucked at geometry in school, even he could see that he needed a longer arc. Looking left and right and hoping local law enforcement was asleep, as well, he backed up until he stood in the middle of the street. Feeling like an idiot, he chose a piece of gravel, rotated his shoulders to loosen them up and aimed at Cate's bedroom window.

Three

Cate groaned and pulled the quilt up around her ears. That stupid squirrel was scratching around in the attic again.

After Isobel's birthday dinner on the mountain, Cate had tucked the old woman into bed as she had promised. Back at her own place, she wandered aimlessly in the bookstore for a long time. She plucked a book off the shelf, read a paragraph or two, replaced it and then repeated the restless behavior.

When she finally went upstairs, it took an hour or more of tossing and turning before she was able to fall asleep. Seeing Brody had unsettled her to a disturbing degree. And now this.

Plink. Plink. The distinctive pinging sound came two more times. And then once more. At last, the veils of slumber rolled away and she understood what was really happening. Brody Stewart. She would bet her signed, first-edition copy of *Gone with the Wind* that it was him.

Grumbling at having to abandon the warm cocoon of covers she had created, she stumbled to the window and looked out. The wavy panes of antique glass were unadorned. There was no one to peek at her from across the street. The owners of the general store used their upstairs square footage for inventory storage. Cate's modesty was safe from this angle, and she liked waking up with the sun.

The moment she appeared at the window, the barrage of gravel stopped. The man down below gesticulated.

Was he insane? Dawn was still hours away. Frowning—and wishing she was wearing something more alluring than flannel—she lifted the heavy wooden sash, leaned out and glared at him. "What do you want, Brody?" She shuddered as icy air poured into the room.

"Come down and unlock the front door. We need to talk."

Was that a socially acceptable way of saying he hoped to end up in her bed? Fat chance. "It's the middle of the night."

"I couldn't sleep. Please, Cate. It's important."

Nothing else he could have said at this hour would have induced her to let the wolf into the henhouse. The truth was, though, they *did* need to talk. Desperately, and soon. Her secret had been weighing heavily on her, and she was running out of time.

"Fine. I'll be down in a minute."

Despite the virtue-protecting properties of flannel,

she wasn't about to meet Brody wearing her nightgown. Grabbing up a pair of jeans and a warm red cashmere sweater, she dressed rapidly and shoved her feet into a pair of fleece-lined slippers. Her hair was a tumbled mess, but she didn't really care. Making herself appear alluring to Brody Stewart was what had gotten her into this wretched state of affairs to begin with.

She didn't turn on any lights as she made her way downstairs. If any of her neighbors were awake, she'd just as soon not have them know she had a late-night guest. Gossip was the bread of life in Candlewick. Cate's personal situation had already edged into the danger zone.

Unlocking the dead bolt and yanking open the door, she shivered and jumped back when Brody burst into the shop. "Damn, it's cold out there," he complained.

"Where's your coat?" In the dark, he was bigger than she remembered from the autumn. More in-your-face masculine.

"I was in a hurry. I forgot it."

"Come on back to the office," she muttered, careful not to brush up against him. "I'll get the fire going."

He followed her down the narrow hallway without speaking and stood in silence as she lit the pile of kindling and wood chips beneath carefully stacked logs. Cate had a handyman who stopped by whenever she asked him—this time of year usually to clean out the grate and restock her woodpile. The fireplace and chimney had been cleaned and inspected regularly, so she had no qualms about using it. Another hearth upstairs in her tiny living room provided warmth and cheer for her apartment.

She wiped her hands on a cloth and indicated one of the tapestry wingback chairs in navy and gold. They were ancient and faded, but the twin antiques had come with the store. She loved them. "Have a seat, Brody. And tell me what's so important it couldn't wait until morning." She would let him speak his piece, and then she would find the courage to tell him the secret she had been hiding from everyone, *including* him.

Brody sat, but his posture indicated unease. She had purposely not turned on the lamps. Firelight was flattering. It also lent a sense of peace and calm to a situation that was anything but. In the flickering glow, Brody's profile was shadowed. Occasionally, when the flames danced particularly high, a flash of light caught the gold in his hair.

He leaned forward, elbows on his knees, and stared at her, his expression impossible to read. "I owe you an apology," he said gruffly.

Her heart thudded. "For what?"

"For what I'm about to say."

Her stomach cringed. "I don't understand."

"Four months ago you and I had something pretty damned wonderful. I'd be lying if I said I didn't want to take you upstairs right now and make love to you for three days straight."

The utter, bald conviction in his words made her light-headed with yearning, but nothing he had said so far erased the certainty of impending doom. "I sense a *but* coming." She kept the words light. It took everything she had. Already her heart was freezing, preparing to shatter.

"But I can't fool around with *you* and still tend to Granny Isobel at the same time. I have a responsibility to discharge."

"How very noble," she mocked, her throat tight with painful tears she couldn't, wouldn't, shed.

His jaw tightened. "I never meant to return. My father was in contact with Granny from the moment I left until last week. Every time he spoke with her she told him things were fine. We assumed she had put the business and the house on the market immediately and would come back to Scotland as soon as the transactions were complete."

"Forgive me for stating the obvious, but I don't think any of you know her very well. It would take a stick of dynamite to blast her out of this town. If she wants to stay, she'll stay."

"Ach, Cate. I ken that very well…now. Do you think you could talk to her? As a favor to me?"

"I could, but I won't. It's not my place. She's my friend. My job is to support her."

"Surely you can see it's time for her to go."

"With you and Duncan…"

"Aye."

"Why couldn't one of you stay here?" Cate was fighting for her future. Isobel's happiness was important, but more was at stake.

Brody shook his head almost violently. "It doesn't make sense. Granny has lived a full and wonderful life. Seasons change, and now her time in Candlewick is done."

"Has anyone ever told you that you're an arrogant, blind, foolish ass of a Scotsman?"

"Don't hold back, Cate."

She leaped to her feet. "Don't worry. I won't." The words she needed to say trembled on her lips. *I'm pregnant, Brody. With your baby.* She had intended—any day now—to send a registered letter to Scotland. Terse. To the point. Morally correct. Absolving him of any responsibility.

It had seemed like a sound plan until Brody showed up in the flesh. Seeing him again was shocking. She hadn't expected to feel so giddy with delight. Nor so bleakly sure that this man was neither the answer to her problems nor the knight on the white horse.

She was still trying to come to terms with the news of her pregnancy. Her periods had never been regular, so she had been twelve weeks along before she went to the doctor and confirmed that her fatigue and queasiness were far more than a temporary condition.

The idea of having a baby had come completely out of the blue, but was not entirely unwelcome. She had always loved children. She was warming quickly to the notion of being a mother. She would do her best to be the kind of warm, nurturing parent she herself had never known. Her mother and father had gone through the motions, but their behavior had been motivated by duty, not gut-deep devotion.

Other worries intruded. What if Brody tried to take their child away from her...insisted the baby live in

Scotland? Was that why she had struggled so over composing the letter? The Stewart-clan pride ran deep, centuries in the making. The mere thought of losing custody made her maternal instincts, hitherto unknown, scratch their way to the surface. She would fight Brody, if need be. She would fight all of them. This baby was hers.

Brody wouldn't be sticking around long this time, perhaps far less than the four weeks he devoted to his grandmother when he visited so soon after the funeral. Clearly, he didn't have any residual feelings for Cate. At least no more than the lust a man feels for a woman he's bedded. Otherwise, he wouldn't be making such a point of not resurrecting their affair.

If she could wait him out, avoid him, stay clear of the family drama, Brody would leave again and Cate would never have to tell him the truth.

She knew in her heart that idea was wrong. A man deserved to know he had fathered a child. Besides, wouldn't Miss Izzy let the cat out of the bag eventually? Cate's elderly friend was far from stupid or naive. She knew her grandson and her neighbor had spent a great deal of time together back in the autumn.

Even if Isobel hadn't guessed before now about Cate and Brody's sexual intimacy, once Cate's belly began to swell visibly, Isobel would do the math and realize that she was going to have another Stewart in the works.

Tension wrapped Cate's skull in a headache. She was an intelligent, educated woman. Surely there was a way forward.

Tell him, her gut insisted. *Tell him*. Postponing the

truth would only make things more difficult. Still, she couldn't bring herself to say the words. What would he say? How would he respond? She felt fragile and helpless, and she hated both emotions.

The baby was only now becoming real to Cate herself. How much more unbelievable would conception seem to Brody? Because Cate's sex life had been nonexistent since moving to Candlewick, she hadn't been taking birth control pills when she met the handsome Scotsman. Brody had been happy to produce a seemingly never-ending supply of condoms.

But there had been that one time in the middle of the night, that poignant, dreamlike coupling, a series of moments as natural as breathing. They had found each other with hushed sighs and ragged groans in the mystical hours when the world slept. She had spread her legs for him, and he had claimed her as his. For all she knew, Brody might not even remember. He'd made love to her many times. Perhaps they all ran together for a man.

Cate remembered each one in vivid detail.

This was not the time to dwell on the past. Nor was it the moment to wallow in grief. She didn't know Brody Stewart well enough to let him break her heart. Love didn't happen so quickly.

She almost believed it.

While she paced, Brody leaned back in his chair, waiting. Judge and jury. He expected Cate to choose his side, to align herself with the grandsons and not Isobel.

If Cate had believed it was the right thing to do, she might have capitulated. Instead, her heart told her she had to fight for the old woman's happiness…and her own. At last, she stopped. She stood at his knees, her arms wrapped around her waist. "Go home, Brody, you and Duncan both. Give her a chance to settle back into the house. Now that she's been up there again, I think she'll quit living over the store."

"And then?"

She shrugged. "Then nothing. You live your life in Scotland. She lives hers here in Candlewick. I'll call you when the time comes."

"When she dies."

"If you want to be blunt about it, yes."

He straightened slowly, unfolding his tall, lanky frame and flexing his wrists until they popped. Despite his self-professed temporary vow of celibacy, he put his hands on her shoulders and massaged them.

Cate couldn't decide if he was attempting to comfort her, or if he was trying to avoid shaking her until her teeth rattled.

Maybe he subconsciously wanted to touch her. She didn't know.

Brody rested his forehead against hers. "You're trying to make me lose my temper, Catie lass, but it won't work. I came here to take care of my grandmother's affairs, and that's what I'm going to do."

"*Your* way."

"It's the *only* way, or at least the only way that makes sense."

His breath was warm on her face. The masculine scent of his skin filled her lungs when she inhaled sharply, imprinting on every cell of her body. Brody was not a man one could easily forget. She leaned into him, blaming her weakness on the late hour and her bone-deep distress. "I won't help you manipulate her, Brody. I won't."

His chest rose and fell in a sigh so deep it made her sad. "I suppose I can understand that. At least promise me you won't be deliberately obstructive. Duncan and I love Granny. We'll take care of her, Cate."

She nodded, her eyes damp. Was it hormones making her weepy or the knowledge that something miraculous had happened? She and Brody had created a baby. People did that every day in every way. But sheer numbers didn't make the awe she felt any less.

With her breasts brushing the hard planes of Brody's chest and her barely-there pregnant tummy nestled against him, she felt an incredible surge of hope mixed with despair. What she wanted from him was the stuff of fairy tales. The gallant suitor. The happy ending.

She made herself step away. "I need to go back to bed," she said. "Please leave."

Brody cupped her cheeks in his big, calloused hands. Years of handling rope and sails had toughened his body. Even without Isobel's estate, Brody's fleet of boats had made him a wealthy man. Isobel had bragged about it often enough. The eventual inheritance would secure his fortune.

His big frame actually shuddered, his arousal impossible to miss. "If it was going to be anybody, it would be you, Cate. But I've never been much for home and hearth."

"Thank you for being honest," she whispered.

Pressing his lips to hers, he kissed her long and deep.

It was a goodbye kiss, bittersweet, painfully bereft of hope. The kind of kiss lovers exchanged on the dock when moviegoers knew the hero was never coming back.

Cate twined her arms around Brody's neck and clung. If this was all she would ever have of him, she needed a memory to sustain her. She could be a single mother. Lots of women did it every day. She wouldn't be any man's obligation.

There was a moment when the tide almost turned. Brody was hard and ready. His hands roved restlessly over her back and settled on her bottom, dragging her close. His hunger made him weak and Cate strong. But she had always been the kind of girl to play by the rules.

Only twice in her life had she broken them, and both times she had paid a high price.

Drawing on a dwindling store of resolve, she released him and eluded his questing hands. "Go," she said. "Go, Brody."

And he did.

Four

Brody spent the following week working himself into a state of physical exhaustion so pervasive and so deep he fell into bed each night and was instantly unconscious. Six months of neglect had left Isobel's spectacular house with a host of issues and problems to be addressed.

He and Duncan made massive lists and checked them off with painstaking slowness. Damaged roofing shingles from a winter storm. Rotting wood beneath a soffit. Gutters clogged with leaves.

Some of the backlog of general repairs dated back to his grandfather's illness. The old man had suffered a stroke five months before he died. Virtually nothing had been done to the house, inside or outside, for almost a year.

Isobel was a wealthy woman. Brody and Duncan

could easily have hired a crew to come in and do everything. But the two grandsons were silently paying penance for not coming sooner and staying longer.

The very depth of their guilt made Brody realize that returning to Scotland *without* their grandmother was going to be unacceptable.

No matter what Cate said, Candlewick was not Isobel's home anymore. Without her beloved American-born husband, she would be far better off to cross the ocean with her two devoted grandsons and settle in amongst the people of her youth.

On the eighth day, Brody and Duncan abandoned the house so a professional cleaning service could descend upon the mountaintop retreat and restore the estate to its previous glory.

While that refreshing and refurbishing was underway, the two men helped Isobel pack up her personal items downtown, everything she had taken with her when she moved into the apartment over her offices.

While Duncan carried a stack of boxes down to the car, Brody sat beside his grandmother and took her hands in his. "You know this is only temporary, Granny…a few nights for you to say goodbye to the house. I contacted a Realtor this morning about preparing the listing."

Isobel Stewart pursed her lips and straightened her spine. Her dark eyes snapped and sparked with displeasure. "I love you dearly, Brody, but you're a stubborn ass, exactly like your father and your grandfather before you. I am neither weak nor senile nor in any kind of physical decline. I'm old. I get it. But my age doesn't give you the right to usurp my decision-making."

Brody ground his teeth. "Duncan and I have lives we've put on hold. We did it gladly, because you're very important to us."

Her fierce expression softened. "I appreciate your concern. I truly do, my lad. But you're making a mistake, and you're being unfair. I'm moving back into my beautiful home—thanks to you boys—but I'm not returning to Scotland. My dear Geoffrey is buried in Candlewick. Everything we built together is here in the mountains. I can't leave him behind. I won't."

"It's dangerous for you to live alone," Brody said, incredulous to realize that he was losing the battle. Isobel would have been far safer to stay here in town where people could keep an eye on her. Now he and Duncan had convinced her to do the very thing they wanted to avoid.

"Life is a dangerous business," the old woman said, her expression placid. "I make my own choices. You can go home with no regrets."

Brody knelt at her side, putting his gaze level with hers. "Please, Granny. For me. Come to Scotland."

She shook her head slowly. "No. I've been away from Scotland too long. Candlewick is my home. Your grandfather and I, together, built something important here… a legacy. We spent so many happy days and months and years creating a host of memories that are all I have left of him. But I might consider a wee compromise if another party is agreeable."

He couldn't imagine any scenario that would make the situation palatable. "Oh?"

His grandmother stood and smoothed the skirt of her black shirtwaist dress that might have been designed anytime in the last six decades. Jet buttons marched all the way up to her chin. "I could ask Cate to move in with me. I'd offer her a modest stipend to be my companion. Keeping a bookstore afloat in the current economic climate is challenging. I'm sure the extra money would help. The girl works herself to death."

Brody bristled inwardly. "I would think Cate's family might help out if she's struggling financially or otherwise. Why does she need you?" Isobel was *his* grandmother, not Cate's.

"You're being churlish. Tell him, Duncan."

Brody's younger brother shut the door to the stairwell and leaned against it, grimacing. "I missed some of that. I love you, Granny. But I have to agree with Brody on this one. We don't want to leave you here in Candlewick all alone, and we can't stay much longer."

Isobel held out her hands. "My idea isn't entirely selfish. Cate has no family of her own. I don't like to divulge her secrets, but you've left me little choice. Her parents are both deceased. They had Cate late in life… an accident."

Brody frowned. "What do you know about them?"

"They were academics. Valued education above all else. I get the impression they were not warm, nurturing people."

"How did she end up in Candlewick?" Brody asked.

"I suggest you ask Cate herself if you want to know. She's a private woman. But I trust her implicitly."

Duncan nodded. "You make a convincing argument. I like Cate. It's not altogether a terrible idea."

Brody glared at his brother. "I thought you were on *my* side, traitor."

Duncan wrapped his grandmother in his arms from behind and rested his chin on top of her gray-haired head. "It's not a war, Brody. I love you both, so don't make me choose. I don't know what the hell is the right thing to do anymore."

Isobel patted his hands and smirked at Brody. "Then I suppose one of you needs to call that very nice caterer and see if he can whip us up another of his wonderful meals this evening. We'll invite Cate to even out the numbers, and after we've plied her with wine and good food, I'll ask her to consider my proposition."

Cate drove up the mountain alone this time. Apparently, Miss Izzy's two grandsons had convinced her to leave her nest above the store.

While Cate applauded acknowledging grief and moving on, it was hard to imagine tiny Isobel sleeping all alone in a six-thousand-square-foot house. Even the thought of it squeezed Cate's heart.

She hadn't wanted to come tonight. The prospect of seeing Brody again turned her bones weak with dread. So many emotions. Guilt. Longing. Wishing for a miracle.

An hour ago she had almost canceled. Suddenly, overnight it seemed, none of her clothes fit. The waistbands of every pair of jeans she owned refused to button. Even her shirts and bras strained to confine her burgeoning breasts. Of course, she wasn't going to head up the mountain in anything but her Sunday best. So she found a loose, long-sleeved knit dress in a modern geometric print of blue and navy hiding in the back of her closet and put it on.

Only the most discerning glance would notice the swell of her pregnant belly. After sliding her feet into low heels and grabbing up a sweater in case the house was drafty, she turned her attention to her hair.

Her instinct was to leave it up in its usual knot on the back of her head. But something told her Brody would see the hairstyle as an in-your-face challenge. They had argued about it often enough. Cate liked her hair to be neat and under control. Brody said it was a sin to hide sunshine from the world.

Despite the current situation, when she remembered their flirtation—barely disguised as squabbles—she had to smile. Feeling Brody's hands in her hair had seduced her as surely as his kisses. He touched her gently but surely, clearly knowing that any token protest on her part was doomed to failure.

When the two of them had lain naked in bed together, Brody played with her hair endlessly. Even now, when she brushed the long, thick mass, she felt a frisson of sensation, of memory, snake down her spine. Most days her hair felt like a burden. When she was with Brody, he made her believe it was a sexy, feminine crowning glory.

Hell's bells. This was not the time to be thinking about Brody. She put a hand to her stomach, flattened her fingers and tried to feel something, anything. Shouldn't she be able to detect the baby moving by now? Were all mothers-to-be this nervous and unsure?

She wanted desperately to have someone else to talk to about her pregnancy. By her deliberate choices, she had no friends in Candlewick close enough to be considered confidantes. Five years ago she had been too wounded and wary to cultivate deep relationships with other women her age. Once she was back on her feet emotionally, she had already gained a reputation as a loner.

Glancing in the mirror, she noted her flushed cheeks and wild-eyed expression. If she didn't get ahold of her pinballing, hormone-driven mental state, both Brody and Duncan, *and* Miss Izzy were going to know something was wrong.

Twenty minutes later she parked in front of Isobel's house, noting with interest, even in the fading light, the way the grounds had been spruced up already. Duncan met her at the door and welcomed her. Was that a deliberate snub on Brody's part? A signal that he'd been very serious about not picking up where they left off?

Perhaps she was being too sensitive. As it turned out, Brody and his grandmother were in the midst of a fiercely competitive game of chess. Duncan and Cate found them in the formal living room, seated on either side of a red-and black-lacquered gaming table.

Geoffrey and Isobel had traveled the world during the course of their marriage. Their home was filled with priceless artwork of all kinds.

Brody looked up when Cate entered the room. He lost his focus momentarily, and Isobel smirked. "Checkmate," she crowed.

"Nice job, Granny," he said absently. He stood and took Cate's hand, lifting it to his lips. "You look stunning, Cate. In fact, if a Scotsman can be forgiven for hyperbole, you glow."

"Thank you," she said, her throat dry. She stepped away and broke his light hold. She couldn't bear to be so close to him with her emotions in turmoil.

The two Stewart brothers were clad in hand-tailored suits and crisp white dress shirts. Duncan's tie was blue. Brody's red. Either man could have graced the cover of *GQ*, but it was Brody whose intense stare made Cate's knees quiver. In more formal clothing, he carried an air of command that was the tiniest bit intimidating.

The other three seemed to be waiting on something. Cate lifted a shoulder. "So what's the occasion? Another birthday? Miss Izzy was very mysterious when she called earlier."

Duncan grinned. If Cate's heart hadn't been otherwise inclined, the younger Stewart brother might have won her over. "We have a proposition for you."

Cate shot Brody a startled glance. "Kinky," she muttered, low enough that Miss Izzy couldn't hear. The old woman's wits were razor-sharp, but her hearing was going.

Brody glared at her. "Behave, Cate. This is serious."

How dare he chastise *her*? "I'm terribly sorry, Mr. Stewart. Please. I'm all ears. What is this mysterious proposition?"

Isobel elbowed her way between her two strapping grandsons and linked her arm with Cate's. "We'll talk about it together over dinner, my dear. Our caterer is amazing, but he's somewhat temperamental. We don't want to keep him waiting."

Forty-five minutes later, with both the soup and salad courses behind them, Cate still hadn't heard anything of substance that warranted this fancy occasion. The food she had eaten rested heavy in her stomach, though it was undoubtedly haute cuisine.

Nerves made her jumpy and tense.

Unfortunately, the Stewart family decided it was a good time to talk about the ubiquitous Scottish dish haggis. Isobel shook her head. "I ate it as a lass, but I'd not be so eager to try it now."

Duncan's grin was mischievous. "What about you, Cate? Would you be game to try our native delicacy?"

Please, God, let them be joking. Surely the American caterer wasn't going that route. She gulped inwardly. "I've heard of it, of course. But to be honest, I'm not entirely sure what it is."

Brody stared at her. "I don't think Cate would be a fan."

"How would you know what I like?" she snapped.

He lifted one supercilious eyebrow. "A sheep's heart, lungs and liver? Chopped up and mixed with onion and oatmeal and all manner of other ingredients…then boiled in the sheep's stomach? Really, Cate? We may not know each other all that well, but you surprise me."

Bile rose in her throat. Her belly heaved in distress. "Oh. Well, no. I suppose not. Sounds revolting."

Duncan took pity on her and changed the subject. The shift gave her a few minutes to breathe and get herself under control. Brody, damn his sorry black-hearted hide, smirked as if he had bested her somehow. Not a chance. Not a damned chance in the world.

While they waited on the main course, Isobel finally grimaced. "Well, lass, here it is. The boys want me to sell out and go back to Scotland. I've let them know unequivocally that I'm not going to do that."

"Oh?" Cate felt as if she were treading a minefield. Neither Duncan nor Brody seemed in any way light-hearted or even at ease about this conversation. Was this some kind of trap for Cate? Did Miss Izzy need Cate to cast a deciding vote?

Isobel nodded, although Cate hadn't really said anything. "I offered a compromise. One the boys believe has merit."

"And that is?"

Izzy smiled gently. "I'd like you to consider moving in here with me as my paid companion. I wouldn't take you away from the bookstore, of course. Your wonderful shop is part of the charm of Candlewick. But my grandsons would feel better knowing that someone was officially looking after me."

"I already do that anyway." Cate frowned. "I care about you, Miss Izzy. And I'm happy to consider moving up here on the mountain with you, but I won't take any money. That's unacceptable."

Brody, the man whose flashing smile was the first thing she had noticed about him months ago, seemed to do nothing but frown at her now. His black scowl pinned her to her chair. "Try not to be difficult, Cate. Granny isn't a charity case. She can afford to pay for in-home help."

Cate was generally even-tempered, but Brody's condescending attitude nicked her on the raw. "Isobel is my *friend*," she said. "It seems to me this is an issue she and I can negotiate on our own. Or perhaps you and Duncan think I'll make the house too crowded."

"Oh, no," Izzy said. "The boys are leaving."

"Leaving?" Cate's tongue felt thick in her mouth. Her stomach clenched. "When?"

Duncan picked up the conversational ball, since his brother was sitting silent and stone-faced with his arms crossed over his chest. "Our tickets are open-ended, but probably in a couple of days. Granny has made up her mind. Since we won't be dealing with real estate issues, we'll head on home and probably make another visit later…in the summer, no doubt."

Cate's skin was clammy and cold, though she felt feverish and overheated from the inside out. Brody was leaving. Dear Lord. What was she going to do? She had to tell him. Or did she?

Perspiration dotted her upper lip. Black spots danced in front of her eyes. "Excuse me," she said. "I'll be back in a moment." She stood up, deathly ill, desperate to make it to the restroom before she broke down in tears.

Humiliation and rage and sheer distress tore her in a dozen directions. Is this what hyperventilation felt like? Nausea rolled through her belly. Not once in her shocking pregnancy had she experienced more than mild discomfort. Now, at the worst possible moment, puking her guts out was a very real possibility.

As she lurched to her feet, her chair wobbled and almost overturned. She grabbed for something, anything. With one hand she gripped the wooden edge of the seat back. With the other, she reached blindly for the table.

"I'm sorry," she whispered. "I don't feel well."

She took a step toward the hallway. Her legs buckled. She heard a trio of shouts. Then her world went black.

Five

Brody leaped to his feet in horror, but he was too late to catch Cate. She crumpled like a graceful swan. Unfortunately, she was close enough to the sideboard to clip her head as she went down. A gash marred her high, pale forehead. "Bloody hell." He crouched beside her, his heart racing in panic. "Get some ice, Duncan."

Isobel sat awkwardly on the floor at Cate's hip. The old woman suffered from advanced arthritis in every joint, but she took one of Cate's hands and patted it over and over again. Her eyes glistened with tears. "Cate. Cate, dear. Open your eyes."

Cate was milk-pale and completely limp and unresponsive. Brody tasted real fear. "Damn it, Duncan! Where's the ice?"

Duncan appeared on the run, out of breath and agitated. "What's wrong with her?" The zip-top plastic bag of ice he carried was wrapped in a thin cotton dish towel.

"Hell if I know. I can't leave her on the floor, though. Hold the ice to her head while I move her." Carefully, Brody scooped Cate up in his arms. She was slender, but tall, so he grunted as he lifted her dead weight. Her gorgeous, sunlit hair cascaded over his arm. The scent of her shampoo and the feel of her feminine body in his arms excoriated him.

Ever since his visit to Cate's bookstore four nights ago, he had second-guessed himself a million times. His decision not to continue their physical relationship seemed like the mature, reasonable choice. It wasn't fair to Cate to pick up where they left off, and what he had told her was true. He needed time with his grandmother. More important, he wasn't a man who had any intention of settling down to family life.

Cate was not a one-night-stand kind of woman.

But God knew, he had vastly underestimated how hard it was going to be to stay away from her now that they were, at least for the moment, living in the same town. He strode down the hallway with only one destination in mind. Entering his bedroom, he motioned for Duncan to throw back the covers.

When that task was accomplished, Brody carefully deposited his precious cargo in his bed.

"Why isn't she waking up?" Isobel fretted.

"She doesn't look good," Duncan pointed out, voicing Brody's own thoughts.

Brody sat and chafed her cool, long-fingered hands.

Duncan kept the ice bag against her temple. Isobel sagged into an armchair, suddenly looking every one of her ninety-two years.

Finally, after what seemed like a lifetime but was probably only another five or ten minutes, Cate's eyelashes fluttered and lifted. Her gaze was cloudy with confusion. "What happened?" she whispered.

Brody smoothed a lock of hair from her cheek. The golden strands clung to his finger. "You fainted."

Though she was ashen before, now she turned dead white, her expression both aghast and defeated. Her throat worked as she swallowed. "Sorry. Didn't mean to scare you."

Duncan moved to the end of the bed. "Could you be coming down with the flu, Cate? I heard in town yesterday that the clinic is seeing a big surge in new cases."

"If that's true," Brody said, "you shouldn't be around Granny. Flu can be deadly for people her age."

Duncan jumped in, clearly trying to temper his brother's unwittingly harsh comment. "Let's not race to conclusions." He smiled gently at Cate. "Do you feel feverish or nauseated?" he asked.

Cate clenched the sheets on either side of her, her fingers gripping the folds white-knuckled. "Yes."

"Damn." Brody gazed down at her, his chest tight. Young people also died from the flu. "I guess we should call the doctor."

Cate struggled to sit up despite their protests. She rested her back against the headboard and pushed the hair from her face. In Brody's big bed she seemed small and lost and defenseless.

Her mouth opened and closed. She licked her dry lips. "I don't have the flu," she said clearly. "I'm pregnant."

Duncan whistled long and slow.

Brody cursed and jerked backward, lurching to his feet. "That's not funny."

Isobel actually laughed and put her hands to her cheeks.

Cate lifted her chin, her eyes glassy with unshed tears. "Do I look like *I* think it's funny?" She turned toward Isobel, who should have been shocked, but instead, sat quietly with a look of Machiavellian concentration on her wrinkled face. "I can still take care of you, Miss Izzy. At least until the baby comes. Don't worry about a thing."

Brody felt his world caving in. "Whose is it?"

Isobel jumped to her feet and thumped his shoulder with all her less-than-substantial weight. "Brody Stewart. You apologize right this instant."

Duncan frowned. "Granny's right."

Brody swallowed hard. Did men faint? He felt damn close himself. He grimaced at his brother and grandmother. "Why don't the two of you go eat before the caterer has apoplexy. Cate and I will stay here and talk."

Cate lurched out of bed. "Oh, no," she cried. "I'm not staying here with *you*." She gave Brody a look that could have melted steel, but the moment she tried to stand, she wobbled and fell over again. This time Duncan caught her, because he was close.

He helped her back onto the bed.

Brody fisted his hands, his chest heaving. "I'm sorry. You two go. Cate and I will be okay."

When Duncan and Isobel exited the bedroom and closed the door, the room fell silent. Brody knew he needed a conciliatory tone, but all he felt was fury and pain. "When were you going to tell me?" he shouted, totally unable to help himself.

Cate shrank back against the headboard, her arms wrapped so tightly around herself it was a wonder she didn't break. "I was working on it," she said, the words dull. "If you don't believe me, feel free to search my laptop. The letter is time- and date-stamped. I started writing it two weeks ago. Right after I found out. You were an ocean away. It wasn't an easy thing to do."

"How far along?" He didn't mean for the question to sound accusatory; he really didn't.

But Cate took it as such. He saw it on her face. "Four months give or take."

"We used protection."

"Not that one time. In the middle of the night."

He blanched, suddenly remembering every detail. He'd awakened hard and aching, already reaching for her in his sleep. She had been like a drug to him. The euphoria of taking her again and again shot him to the top and wrung him out. He'd been obsessed with her.

If he hadn't gone back to Scotland, they might have fucked themselves to death.

"Is there a chance anyone else could be the father?" He made himself ask the dreadful question.

Cate's green eyes sheened with tears. "Of course not, you stupid, thickheaded Scotsman." Her voice was tight. "If I weren't about to throw up on your priceless oriental rug right now, I'd get out of this bed and slug you in the stomach. Do you really think I found someone else so quickly after you left? Good Lord, Brody. You were the first man I'd slept with in five years. And that was a fluke. I wasn't looking for sex in the first place."

He knew she tried to stifle the sob at the end, but it slipped out. Why was he being such a prick? Perhaps because he had never been so scared and confused and guilty in his life. And ashamed. Conscience-stricken that he hadn't been with her during these traumatic weeks.

"Have you been sick from the beginning?" The only way to establish any sense of normalcy was to keep talking, but honest to God, his head spun, and he hadn't a clue what to do. It was like the time he took one of his boats out alone and got caught up in a wicked storm and nearly drowned.

Only tonight was much worse.

Cate shook her head slowly. "No. This is new."

He scraped both hands through his hair, trying and failing to come to terms with the fact that he was going to be a father. Nothing made sense.

"I'll provide for the child," he said, his jaw clenched so hard his temples screamed with pain.

Cate's emerald eyes went dark. "You needn't bother with speeches, Brody. The only reason I was going to tell you about the baby at all was to soothe my conscience. I make a decent living. I have a nest egg from my parents. I don't want or expect anything from you. You're free to go back to Scotland. The sooner, the better, in fact. Isobel doesn't need you and neither do I."

Fury, hot and wild, pounded in his veins. But when

he looked at her, sitting so defeated and miserable in his bed, he forced himself to swallow the words of angry confrontation that he wanted to throw at her. Cate carried his child. She was sick and confused and vulnerable.

"Clearly, there are decisions to be made," he said quietly. "Now is not the time. I know you don't feel well, but you need to eat. Let's go back to the dining room and give it a try."

"You go," she said stubbornly. "I'll stay here and rest."

He managed a smile and wondered if it seemed as strained and false as it felt to him. "I can tell you're feeling better," he said. "Your cheeks have color in them again. Don't fight me on this, Cate. You'll only make things worse."

Ignoring her sputtered protests, he kissed her on the forehead and picked her up again. "You'll wear yourself out fighting, Little Mama. Take a break tonight. Talk to Duncan and Granny. Tomorrow the sun will come up and you'll feel better, I swear. We both will."

Her head lolled against his shoulder, her breath warm on his neck. "I hate you, Brody."

A mighty sigh lifted his chest and rolled through him with a tsunami of regrets. "I know, Cate. I know."

An hour later Brody stood at the front door and watched as the taillights of Cate's car disappeared down the hill. He had lost the violent argument about whether or not she would drive herself back to town. Only when brave, beautiful Cate broke down in tears did he make himself back down. He didn't know much about pregnant women, but her mental state seemed precarious at the moment, so he acquiesced reluctantly. It felt like an eternity before he at last got her text saying she was safely at home.

The caterer was long gone and the countertops pristine. Brody prowled the darkened kitchen, scrounging in the refrigerator for a piece of the key lime pie he had been too upset to eat earlier.

Though it was late, Brody was miles away from feeling sleepy. Maybe he was finally getting over his jet lag, and maybe tonight's news would give him permanent insomnia. Adrenaline pumped in his veins. He jumped when Duncan showed up unannounced in the dimly lit space.

Duncan sprawled in a cane-bottomed chair at the small table in the breakfast nook. "What are you going to do?"

That was Duncan. Cut to the chase. Don't dance around the issue.

"I haven't a clue," Brody said sullenly. "What would you do in my shoes?"

"Cate is an intelligent, beautiful, fascinating woman."

It pissed Brody that Duncan had noticed. Caveman instincts he didn't know he possessed clubbed their way to the speech center of his brain. "Don't get any ideas, little brother."

Duncan made a rude hand gesture. "If you don't want her, why shouldn't she find another guy who will value and appreciate her?"

Brody's teeth-grinding headache was back. "I never said I didn't want her."

"Oh, come on, Brody. I know you pretty damn well.

You never date any woman long enough for her to get ideas about marriage. You might as well have it tattooed on your forehead. *Brody Stewart doesn't commit.*"

It was true. In fact, Brody had given Cate a version of the same speech. "You make me sound like a jackass."

"If the kilt fits."

"Very funny."

"Do you think there's any possibility she got pregnant on purpose? To force your hand?" Duncan's look held enough real sympathy to make Brody's throat tighten.

Brody swallowed hard. "No. Zero possibility. It was all on me." He'd made a mistake. A passion-driven, unthinking, hot and crazy, erotic mistake. That one unbearably sensual night had been emblematic of the two-week affair he couldn't forget. Now there was going to be a far more tangible reminder of his impulsive, testosterone-driven behavior.

Panic rose again, tightening his chest. "I don't know what to do, Duncan. Swear to God, I don't."

Duncan rolled to his feet and got a beer from the fridge. He popped the cap. "What do you *want* to do?"

"I want to rewind my life and go back to last week."

"Not an option, bro."

"You're no help."

"Look at it this way. We were both planning to go home in a few days. Now you can stay and make sure Granny is doing okay."

"I don't want to stay," Brody yelled, tempering the volume at the last minute to keep from awakening his grandmother.

"Then come back to Scotland with me. I'm sure Cate can manage without you."

Hearing the stark choices laid out so succinctly made Brody's blood chill. He glared. "Sometimes I wish I could still knock the crap out of you like I did when we were teenagers," he muttered.

"Your memory is faulty. I won at least half of those skirmishes. Face it, Brody. You're not the first guy to find yourself in this situation, and you won't be the last. But Granny complicates the equation. She won't let you walk away from your responsibilities."

"I appreciate your high opinion of me."

Duncan shrugged. "You live on another continent. Cate will do fine on her own. I, of all people, would understand if you set up a trust fund and let that be it. Do you even like kids?"

"How would I know? I could learn, I guess."

"I think the bigger question is whether or not Cate Everett means more to you than an easy lay." Duncan yawned. "I've got to get some sleep," he said, standing and tossing the empty bottle in the recycle bin. "I'll do whatever I can to help, Brody. But the first move is yours."

Six

Now that Cate had fallen prey to pregnancy sickness, it settled in with a vengeance. The morning after the disastrous dinner party, she was late opening the store because she spent an hour hunched over the sink in the tiny antiquated bathroom of her upstairs apartment. Fortunately, tourists were not beating down her door in late February. Most people in town were busy with their own endeavors.

By the time she made it downstairs midmorning, the worst of the nausea had passed. Until noon, she was able to huddle by the fire and sip a cup of tepid tea and think. Apparently, *pregnancy brain* must be a real thing, because random thoughts bounced inside her skull like a drunken pinball game.

She was an inveterate list-maker as a rule. Though a

blank pad lay on the table at her elbow, and a nearby antique coffee tin held an assortment of pens, she never actually wrote down anything at all. The future stretched before her, a terrifyingly blank canvas.

Would she set up a nursery in Miss Izzy's house? That wasn't part of the deal. It was a lot to ask of a woman Isobel's age to welcome an infant with all of the accompanying inconveniences and demands.

And what about the store? Would Cate have to find a manager? Could she afford to take maternity leave? It would be five years before the kid went to kindergarten.

At the moment an eerie and surprising calm wrapped her in a soothing cocoon. One hand rested on her stomach. This pregnancy was real. But she didn't feel any different. If it wasn't for the nausea, she could easily ignore the entire fiasco.

Only when she allowed herself to think about Brody Stewart did pain intrude. If there had ever been a man less pleased to hear he was going to be a father, she couldn't imagine it.

Brody had reacted to her news with shock and dismay and even anger. She winced inwardly, remembering his face. She couldn't really blame him. This situation was unprecedented for both of them.

To be honest, it was probably best he lived an ocean away. There would be no awkward encounters on the street, no need to take his feelings into account when she began making decisions about what kind of baby bed to buy, how soon to introduce solid foods and when to decide the kid was old enough for day care.

She didn't want or need Brody to take up parenting as a duty. No child deserved that. Neither did Cate.

Cate was in this all alone…for the duration. At least she had five more months to get used to the idea. The baby would be born in July. That was good. No worries about blizzards or nasty winter viruses. She would be able to go for long walks with the baby in the stroller and get back in shape after pregnancy strained her body.

She wanted to be elated and excited and exuberant about her situation. And she would be…probably. As soon as she got beyond feeling so sick and tired and overwhelmed. She hoped so.

She had actually dozed off in her chair when the bell over the front door jingled. With a yawn, she stood up and stretched. "Coming," she said. For some reason, finding Brody standing near the cash register caught her completely off guard. "What are you doing here?"

He lifted an eyebrow. "We have decisions to make."

Her heartbeat sped up drunkenly. "No," she said carefully. "*We* don't have to decide anything. This is my baby. All I owed you was the courtesy of information. Now that we have that out of the way, you're off the hook. Fly home with your brother."

He scowled. "I think we should get married."

She swallowed, and her eyes bugged out. "Um, no. Let's not do the dance, Brody. You have nothing to worry about. I've got this. Your boats need you."

"You and I are good together in bed."

The blunt challenge angered her and at the same time made her legs quiver. Heavens, yes. They definitely were. But so what? That didn't make a marriage. "And your point?"

"Lots of couples start with far less."

She rubbed two fingers in the center of her forehead. "A hundred years ago I'm sure there were shotgun weddings all over North Carolina. But, thank God, that's in the past. No one will bat an eye if I have this baby on my own. Seriously, Brody. You owe me nothing, nothing at all."

"You're carrying my baby." His gaze was stormy.

"But you don't really want to be a father, do you? Be honest. You don't even want to be a husband. Why would we put ourselves through a sham that will only lead to heartbreak?"

His brooding stare made her nipples tighten against the slippery fabric of her bra. She had never met a man as unflinchingly masculine as Brody Stewart. It was easy to imagine him in another time, a fiery chieftain leading his clan.

"I can't win this particular argument," he said, "since I was so blatant about not wanting to settle down and be a family man. But circumstances have changed, Cate."

"Not for you. Not really. I won't be an obligation you check off some moral list, Brody."

"Would marrying me be such a terrible fate?"

In his deep blue eyes, she saw a hint of the same turmoil she had carried with her every day since the baby became a reality. The prospect of being Brody Stewart's bride was a fantasy she had entertained briefly back in the fall. The intensity of their combustible attraction had raised the possibility that Brody might be *the one*.

Even now it would be far too easy to fall prey to the fairy tale. But she had done that once before and been burned. She was older...wiser.

Fortunately, more bookstore enthusiasts arrived, erasing any possibility of further substantive conversation.

Brody's lips tightened with frustration, but he waited more or less patiently as she greeted her customers. Then he caught her by the arm and drew her close. "I'll take you to dinner tonight. In Claremont. We'll talk."

Claremont was the next town over. Bigger. More cosmopolitan. Lots of lovely restaurants. "It won't change anything," she said.

He curled an arm around her waist and dragged her closer for one hard kiss. "Wear something nice," he said. "I'll pick you up at six."

The weather had finally moderated. The day was sunny with a hint of spring warmth. The hours crawled by, but at last Cate was free to put the *closed* placard in the front window and lock the doors.

Upstairs, she dithered over what to wear. Brody had taken her to eat in Claremont several times back in the fall. If he chose their favorite spot again, she would need to dress for the ambiance.

The only nice outfit she owned—that still fit—was a red jersey tank dress that left her shoulders bare. Her newly burgeoning breasts swelled against the scooped neckline. Pairing the sexy number with a sober black wool shawl would keep her warm and at the same time lend respectability to the above-the-knee frock. She didn't want to give Brody any ideas.

The larger-than-life Scotsman was punctual. It was one of the many things she liked about him. That and the way he charmed everyone they met, from strangers on the street to clerks and servers and anyone else who crossed his path. His thick, whiskey-colored hair, broad-shouldered masculinity and bone-melting accent were a trifecta that won over even the most curmudgeonly of acquaintances.

As he helped her into the car with a solicitous touch, she told herself she wouldn't be dazzled by something as shallow as sex appeal. So the man had a great smile and smelled like a crisp alpine forest. That wasn't enough. She was going to be a mother. She had mature decisions to make. Sex would only cloud the process.

Brody, perhaps correctly reading her reluctance, was on his best behavior. During the twenty-mile drive, they discussed movies and books and Isobel's determination to remain in her home.

Cate smiled. "It's hard for me to believe that one tiny old lady can stand up to a duo of strapping Scotsmen."

"We can't exactly tote her over our shoulder and kidnap her onto a plane. Granny has made up her mind. It complicates things for the family down the road, but we love her. Our father was naive to believe Duncan and I could sway her. But then again, none of us realized how much she loves it here in North Carolina. With Grandda gone, I thought Candlewick would hold too many painful memories."

"It's the memories that keep her going, I think."

"Seems so."

When they arrived at the restaurant, serious conversation was tabled for the moment. The tuxedo-clad host actually remembered them. He bent over Cate's hand with a theatrical French flair. "We are honored to have such a beautiful woman grace our humble restaurant."

The *humble* restaurant had three Michelin stars and an extensive wine cellar, so Cate took his effusive greeting with a grain of salt. "It's good to be back," she said.

Brody's lips twitched, but she gave him points for not rolling his eyes. The host seated them at a prime table in the corner near a large window that looked out over a scenic pond. Gardens, still clad in drab winter colors, nevertheless beckoned with tiny white lights strung in the branches of budding trees.

The last time she and Brody had patronized this particular establishment, they took a walk after dinner. He had pulled her into the shadows and kissed her desperately. They'd been so hungry for each other that the trip back to Candlewick had seemed endless.

The memory brought no pleasure. Cate had been giddy with infatuation back then. But soon after, Brody disappeared from her life.

Her dinner companion picked up on her wistful mood. After they ordered he leaned back in his chair and stared at her. "What's wrong? I thought this place was a favorite of yours."

She shrugged. "It was. It is. If I'm not mistaken, though, this is where you and I spent the evening before we went back to my place and…well, you know. Made a baby."

His face changed. "Ah, hell, lass. I'm sorry."

"It doesn't matter." Clearly, Brody didn't remember every moment of their affair.

The entrées arrived, derailing the awkward pause. Cate's stomach cooperated long enough for her to eat grilled salmon and sautéed squash. Brody's smile had gotten lost somewhere along the way. He consumed most of a strip steak and a baked potato, but his jaw was firm and his gaze hooded.

At last, the meal was done. Cate put down her fork and pulled her shawl more tightly around her shoulders. The restaurant wasn't cold, but she needed something to hold on to. She inhaled sharply. "Here's the thing, Brody. When and if I ever get married, I want it to be to a man who loves me and wants to be with me always. You're not that guy."

He couldn't argue the point. Not when he had so very carefully told her he wasn't interested in picking up where they left off.

"Circumstances have changed." He spoke carefully as if he was looking for exactly the right words to convince her.

"It doesn't matter. *You* haven't changed. I deserve better than a reluctant husband and father."

He winced. "I said a lot of things recently. Maybe I was a fool." He reached across the table and took one of her hands in his. His thumb stroked the pulse at the back of her wrist. "We could make it work, lass. For the baby."

Cate shivered inwardly. She could fall in love with Brody Stewart so easily. When he went back home last

October, her world had gone flat for a while. The autumn leaves had seemed duller, the blue skies not as vibrant. Even the crisp mornings and warm afternoons—normally her favorite season of the year—had failed to lift her spirits.

Brody had crashed into her humdrum existence with the force and heat of a meteorite. She could no more have resisted his brash Scottish charm than she could have stopped the sun from coming up. He had wanted her and she had wanted him. They had wallowed in their mutual, intense attraction.

When he left, the physical realities of a harsher-than-normal North Carolina mountain winter had echoed the aching loss in her soul.

Having Brody, even briefly, and then losing him had hurt. A lot. Why would she ever let herself be so vulnerable again?

She pulled her hand away. Touching him or vice versa was dangerous. "We created a baby in a moment of physical need. It happened. I don't blame you. You're a nice man. You're honest. You care about your grandmother. If I thought you had any long-term interest in this child, I would make sure you could see him or her now and again. But be honest, Brody. You don't want to take on that kind of emotional responsibility for the rest of your life…do you?"

"I haven't had much time to think about it."

It wasn't an answer. Not really.

Perhaps she owed him more of her life than she had shared up until now. Maybe it would help him understand. "I know what it's like to be a child who's not wanted."

His face reflected shock. "You?"

"Yes. I wasn't an orphan. So you don't have to feel sorry for me. That's not the point of this story. My parents were both college professors. Sociologists. They chose not to have children because they wanted to be free to travel the world and research indigenous populations in remote places. They knew it wouldn't be fair to leave a child behind for someone else to raise."

"So what happened?"

"When my mother was forty-nine years old and approaching menopause, she found out she was pregnant. Needless to say, it was a shock. She and my father were good, decent people. They didn't give me up for adoption. Instead, they put an end to their travels and settled into teaching year-round."

"But they resented you…"

His attempt to understand was almost comical. "Nothing so dramatic. They did everything parents are supposed to do. There were nannies, of course, when I was an infant and toddler, but good ones. When I was old enough for kindergarten, my mother and father began attending parent/teacher conferences and school programs."

"I don't understand."

"They were going through the motions. One reason they never wanted children was because they weren't 'kid' people, and they knew that about themselves. Instead of warmth and hugs and genuine parent/child bonding, it was more like playacting. They tried their best to perform the assigned roles, I really believe that, but it was a hollow effort."

"How old were you when you realized?"

An insightful question. Brody was sharp and intuitive.

"Seven, I think. That would have been the spring of first grade. My class put on a play. We had a dress rehearsal one Saturday morning, because we were to perform for the whole school the following Monday. On the day of practice, there were parents everywhere… laughing, talking, taking photographs. My best friend's mother brought cupcakes for everyone. Another kid's father videotaped the practice."

"And your parents?"

"They sat on folding chairs in a back corner of the auditorium. Never spoke to anyone. Never involved themselves in the chaos. I know I was very small, and it's possible I've embellished the details, but what stands out in my memory is the look of discomfort on their faces. Maybe that was the first time they realized they had committed themselves to more than a decade of this kind of thing."

"I'm sorry, Cate." Brody's gaze was troubled.

"Don't be. Over the years I came to understand that I was luckier than some. I had every material advantage and a safe place to sleep at night."

"Children need love."

"Yes, they do. That's what I'm trying to tell you. If babies aren't your thing, it would be best for all of us if we come to terms with that now."

Brody ignored her pointed advice. He drummed his

fingers on the linen tablecloth. "What about the rest of your life?"

"I did well in school. Didn't make waves. When I went off to college, I think it was a relief for all three of us. My parents were finally free to live life as they pleased, and I was ready to be an adult."

"Granny told me your parents died before you came to Candlewick…is that right?"

"Yes. My father was diagnosed with lung cancer six years ago. One afternoon when my mother was driving him home from a doctor's appointment, a drunk driver ran a red light. They were killed instantly."

"Damn, Cate. I'm so sorry."

Her throat tightened to a painful degree. "Thank you. But it was a very long time ago. I grieved and moved on."

Brody frowned. "You and I could provide emotional security for this baby. I have family to share and to spare. It makes perfect sense for you to marry me."

"Stop pushing me," she said. "You think you can make everything work out simply by willing it to be the way you want it, but life is not that easy. Emotions are messy and complicated. Babies even more so…"

Seven

Brody lifted a hand to summon the waiter. He wanted to pay the check and get out of this place. Hearing Cate's story haunted him. His own family saga wasn't much better. But at least his parents had been physically affectionate. Even if they hadn't been able to stay married to each other, neither of their sons had ever doubted they were loved.

On the steps of the restaurant, he put a hand beneath Cate's elbow. "Do you feel like walking? It's a beautiful night."

Beneath his fingertips, he felt her stiffen. But a moment later she murmured an affirmative. As they descended the steps, Cate's elegant shawl caught on a nail and slipped out of her grasp. Before he could retrieve it, another guest picked it up and returned it.

"Thanks," Brody said. When he swiveled back to Cate, his eyes widened. She had kept a death grip on her simple wrap the entire evening. This was the first time he had seen her without the shawl. He remembered the red dress from before. What he didn't recall were the voluptuous curves plumped up on display above the neckline. "Holy hell."

She crossed her arms defensively. "Yes," she said wryly. "I've got boobs now. Put your eyes back in your head."

He swallowed and carefully tucked the soft wrap around her shoulders. "You had beautiful breasts before, lass. Now there's simply more of you to admire."

Cate laughed. He hadn't realized how much he missed that sound. Things were so serious between them now. "Come on," he said gruffly. "Exercise is good for pregnant women."

"How would you know?"

He wrapped an arm around her waist and steered her down the path of small, smooth stones. "I downloaded a pregnancy manual on my iPad. I've made it to chapter three so far."

Cate stopped dead in the middle of the walkway and stared up at him. "You can't be serious."

Her incredulity stung. "This is important to me, Catie girl. It might not be what I wanted, but it's what I've got...what *we've* got. It pays to be prepared. I have a responsibility to you." He brushed a gentle fingertip over the wound on her head. "You've already passed out once," he muttered. "We can't let that happen again."

She had covered the abrasion with makeup, but he could still see the swelling.

"I'll admit the knot does ache, but pain reliever helped, so it's nothing to worry about. Last night was stressful. I'm fine now. Honestly."

"We'll see."

Apparently, that annoying phrase translated across the globe. "Don't try to *handle* me, Mr. Stewart. I'm not one of your boats."

He chuckled, linking his hand with hers and squeezing her fingers. They strolled along in harmony. "Do you even like the water, Cate?"

"I don't dislike it," she said.

"I'd enjoy taking you sailing, lass. I have a honey of a boat called the *Mary Guinn*. She's sleek and fast and responds to my hand on the wheel like a cloud dancing across the sky. There's nothing like being out on the loch with the breeze whipping the water into a frenzy and the sun on your face. It's poetry, lass. Pure poetry."

"So is this Mary person a former lover?"

"No. But she *was* my first teenage crush. Two years older than me and sweet as a spoonful of honey. I was madly in love with her for an entire spring."

"She must have been really something to inspire you to name a boat after her."

He stopped and pulled her to face him, holding her narrow shoulders between his two hands. "Are ye jealous, Cate?"

Her chin lifted. "Of course not. Don't be absurd."

He hadn't meant to kiss her. Not tonight. Not with so

much at stake. But the way her wary green eyes gazed up at him lit a fire in his belly. "God, I've missed you."

He slid his hands beneath her hair and cupped her head, diving in deep for the first kiss, then lingering and savoring the second. He'd half expected her to slap his face and run away. Instead, she leaned into him and curled her arms around his neck.

"I missed you, too, Brody."

This time when the shawl fell, neither of them cared. His hands shook. How had he made himself believe he could stay away from this woman? Even with an ocean between them he had remembered the way her body fit his so perfectly. Was that a happy coincidence or a portent of something greater?

Tongue tangling with hers, he breathed raggedly. In his arms, she felt like home. "Do ye believe in fate, Catie girl? The Scots are a superstitious people. We come from a long line of seers and prophets. Sometimes life steers us in ways we're meant to go."

She pulled back for a moment, her lips swollen from his kisses, her cheeks flushed. The moonlight painted her in silver. "Don't make something out of nothing, Brody. Sex is sex. It doesn't mean we're the folk heroes of a Celtic legend. I like sleeping with you. You knocked me up. End of story."

He put a hand over her mouth. "Don't talk like that. You're not meant to be flippant."

She nipped his fingers with sharp teeth. "For a man who said 'no more sex' in no uncertain terms, you're creating a very compromising situation."

Cate was right. They had wandered about as far away

from the restaurant as it was possible to go. No one could see them here in the copse of trees unless they stumbled upon them. And that was unlikely. Other diners were inside keeping warm.

He ran his hands up and down her arms. "I want ye badly, lass. I don't know what I was thinking."

"Did you sleep with other women when you went home?"

The question knocked the wind out of him.

Cate clapped a hand over her mouth, her expression aghast. "Forget I said that, Brody. It's none of my business."

He was stunned. Not by her question, but by his own calculations. He'd told himself the boat business had kept him too busy over the winter to get laid. What a pile of horseshit. Apparently, he'd not actually been tempted by any of the women who crossed his path. None of them had been Cate.

"The answer is no," he said bluntly.

She went still. "Really?"

He shrugged. "Really."

"Then why the big speech last week?"

"Maybe I'm a damned fool. Come here, little Cate. Let me kiss you again."

She put a hand in the center of his chest, holding him momentarily at bay. "I'm five foot ten. Not little at all. And I won't let you coerce me with sex. This baby is none of your business."

"I'll be honest, woman. Right now I've no' got a thought for anything but touching you." He shimmied her skirt up to her hips. "Damn, your skin is soft." He was losing control. He recognized his fraying resolve. Tonight was supposed to be about solving the mess he had made. Now he was perilously close to compounding his transgressions.

"Brody…" She whispered his name with such yearning the hair on his nape stood up.

His next discovery fried his reasoning. "Lord, God, woman. Are you no' wearing any underwear?" She had gooseflesh all over, so he shrugged out of his suit jacket and tucked it around her.

"It's a thong," she muttered. "It keeps me from having lines in my dress."

He wrapped his fingers in the tiny sliver of satin and ripped it with a satisfying jerk. "No lines at all, my sweet. You're welcome."

Scooping her up, he urged her legs around his waist and backed her against the nearest tree, knowing his coat would protect her skin. "Tell me to stop, and I'll stop." It would kill him, but he would. He'd already changed Cate's life irrevocably with this pregnancy. He needed to know what she expected from him.

She cupped his face in her hands. "I want you to quit talking, Brody. Hurry. Before someone finds us out here."

Although Cate didn't get the words exactly right, she had her hand on his zipper, so he was definitely clear about where this was going.

What happened next was both clumsy and exhilarating. With both of them breathless and urgent and trying to help the other, at last he was inside her. "Ah, damn, my Cate."

"Brody, Brody…" She clung to him tightly.

Except for her bunched-up dress and his still-buttoned shirt, they were as close as two humans could be. He caressed her smooth, firm bottom. "Is it weird that I'm really turned on 'cause you're pregnant?"

Her laugh was a choked gasp. "I don't think so. Besides, I don't *feel* pregnant. All I can think about is how long it's been since we did this."

"Too long," he groaned. Already he was close to coming, and that was unacceptable.

Cate bit his earlobe and whispered something naughty in his ear. His temperature shot up a hundred and fifty degrees. "Stop that," he pleaded. "I'm trying to make this last."

Cate shivered hard. It was far too cold to be fooling around outside, but she didn't care. Brody was making love to her. So many lonely nights she had dreamed of this. When she told herself time and again that the sex couldn't have been as earth-shattering as she remembered, she tried to believe that was so. Only now Brody was back and the truth stared her in the face.

Whatever this was between them was magic.

His big, ruggedly masculine body radiated heat despite the air temperature. Each time he moved in her, the hard length of him probed sensitive spots that made her close her eyes and arch her back, aching for something just out of reach.

Even in the midst of physical euphoria, her brain offered irritating explanations. Probably Brody was using this interlude to coax her into doing things his way. He thought if they were lovers, she would say yes to him across the board.

She shoved away the unwelcome thoughts. His strength made her feel intensely feminine. Despite her years of education and her dedication to women's empowerment, the fact that he was able to hold her so easily spoke to some deep unevolved corner of her psyche.

Brody was a protective male. He would keep her safe if she allowed it.

He muttered her name and rested his forehead against hers. His big body quaked. "I've lost my bloody mind."

His coffee-scented breath was warm on her cheek. She wanted to gobble him up. "Are you complaining, Brody?" She squeezed him intimately with inner muscles.

"No," he croaked. "Never." He adjusted the jacket he had wrapped around her. "Am I hurting you?"

The tree bark had scraped her hip bone when the coat fell, but she barely noticed. "I'm good."

He pulled back and reached between their joined bodies to give her the extra bit of stimulation she needed to hit the peak. "Come for me, lass."

She was primed and ready. The sweet tide rolled through her and left her limp in his arms. Brody thrust his way to completion moments later and heaved a great sigh, his body shuddering in the aftermath.

In the echoing silence that followed, Cate yawned unexpectedly. The intense fatigue of early pregnancy sapped her energy. Under the circumstances, Brody had taken whatever bit of strength she had left.

He chuckled and carefully disengaged their bodies, setting her on her feet and holding her arm until she was steady. She had lost a shoe, so they had to scramble in the dark to find it. She leaned against him, replete, weary, oddly unconcerned about the future. Just being near him gave her a deep sense of peace.

She didn't examine those feelings too intently. It was difficult enough to come to terms with impending motherhood. She didn't have the mental fortitude to deal with how Brody fit into the picture.

He insisted on carrying her back to the car, which was embarrassing and sweet, and yet in some odd way, frightening. He'd been back in Candlewick such a short time, and already she was letting him take charge.

That couldn't happen.

Like a famous Southern heroine, Cate would think about it tomorrow.

Back at the bookstore, they argued. Brody wanted to come upstairs and spend the night. Cate needed space and time to think.

She faced him on the sidewalk, wrapped once again in her cozy black shawl. "You said it first, Brody," she pointed out. "We shouldn't and *can't* pick up where we left off last October. You have concerns about helping your grandmother, but now I have responsibilities, too."

He cursed beneath his breath, his grumpy displeasure evident. "So what happened back there at the restaurant? Or in the woods, to be more exact."

Cate shrugged, feeling tears prick her eyes. This hormonal roller coaster made it difficult to be wise. "We lost our heads. It was nice to be together again. Maybe you were trying to sway me to your way of thinking."

He put a finger under her chin and tipped her face

up to his. In the glow of the streetlight, his eyes flashed with temper. "I didn't make love to you to win points, Cate. I hadn't planned for that to happen at all. But I'm not sorry."

"I'm not asking for an apology."

"Then what do you want from me?"

"My life is changing whether I want it to or not. I'll move up to the house and stay with Miss Izzy. You and Duncan can feel free to go home."

"And what about the baby?"

"I'll figure it out."

Brody knew he had made a major misstep. Earlier— before picking Cate up for dinner—he had realized sex would cloud the issue, but he hadn't been able to help himself. It had been so long, so damn long, since he left Candlewick. He'd been away for sixteen, seventeen weeks, give or take, and in all that time, Cate Everett had been an incandescent memory haunting his dreams.

The drive back up the mountain was relatively short. Certainly not enough time to unravel the many challenging aspects of his current situation.

He hadn't even kissed her good-night, damn it. Cate had unlocked the bookshop door and slipped inside, leaving him to stand on the street like some lovesick adolescent and wait for her bedroom light to come on so he would know she was okay.

When he finally pulled up in front of his granny's house and got out of the car, the last person on earth he wanted to see was his brother. Apparently, Duncan had been waiting up for him. They stood outside on the driveway, speaking in low voices.

Duncan didn't mince words. "I'm packed for my flight out tomorrow morning. Have you decided if you're coming with me?"

Brody thought about his fleet of beautiful and sturdy boats, and his comfortable house in the glen, and the way his buddies gathered at the local pub at the end of the week to share a pint and celebrate everything or nothing at all. He slammed a fist on the hood of the car. "I can't leave. Not yet. Nothing is settled."

"You don't think Cate can deal with this on her own? She has Granny, and Cate strikes me as an eminently capable woman."

"It's *my* baby," Brody said. Why did no one understand that?

Duncan shrugged. "One lucky sperm doesn't make you father of the year. Don't break Cate's heart, Brody. Right now you're caught up in wanting to make a grand gesture. Ye've got to think carefully, man."

"Would you leave if you were me?" The words came out sharp and angry, taking Brody by surprise. He hadn't known his mood was so volatile.

The silence stretched from seconds to minutes. Duncan leaned against the side of the car, his gaze focused somewhere out in the dark night. At last, he sighed and faced Brody. "I can't say for sure. But I think it would depend more on the baby's mother than the kid itself. I saw how you looked at Cate. Are you in love with her?"

Brody felt his face heat and was glad Duncan couldn't see. "Of course not. I barely know her."

"Looks like you know her plenty well to me." The comeback was wry and pointed.

"People have sex without being in love."

"Aye. So I'll rephrase the question. Do you think Cate is in love with you?"

Eight

Do think Cate is in love with you? Duncan's question haunted Brody for hours. When the sun came up, he had barely slept. He drove Duncan to the airport.

Once his brother had checked in and was ready to go through security, Brody hugged him tightly. "Thanks."

Duncan lifted an eyebrow and smiled, not appearing to notice the female TSA official who was giving him the eye. "What did I do?"

"Ye're family. The best part, in fact. Are you sure you're willing to take over the business for a few weeks?" He'd told Duncan at breakfast that he was going to stay in Candlewick until important decisions were made.

"I already handle all the boring business part," Duncan said, grinning. "I think I can survive the rest."

"I love you, man." Surely that wasn't panic slugging through his veins. Duncan was making a clean getaway. Brody was trapped.

Duncan picked up his carry-on and cuffed his brother on the shoulder. "You'll figure this out, Brody. I have complete faith in you."

When Brody's last and most final connection to Scotland walked away and disappeared into a queue of travelers, Brody returned to his car and made the drive back to Candlewick. When it had been the two of them arriving ten days ago, Brody had been confident and buoyed by the knowledge that a duo of Stewart men could deal with just about anything.

Now here he was, all alone. Duncan was happily bound for Scotland. Granny wasn't going *anywhere*. And Cate Everett was pregnant with Brody's baby. God help him.

When he made it back to his grandmother's house, he found her in the study going through a drawer of her husband's private correspondence. "Well," he said, forcing cheer, "Duncan's on his way home."

Isobel stood up from the desk and stretched. "Ye look half sick, my boy. Things will all work out."

So much for pretending. "What are you up to, Granny?" he asked, ignoring the subject he didn't want to discuss.

She grimaced. "Trying to decide what to pack away and what to pitch. Your grandda was a dab hand with pen and words. I see his beautiful, spidery writing, and I want to keep every scrap of paper." She ran a hand across the smooth cherry of the desk. "It's daft, I know."

He hugged her and then sprawled on the love seat. "Not daft. Not at all. There's no rush, is there?"

"Not really, but with our Cate moving in, I thought it would be a nice gesture to give her this office. So she could deal with bookstore matters and not go to town every single day."

Brody frowned. "You think she'll close the shop occasionally?"

"It's already closed on Sundays and Mondays. That's when she normally does her accounting and ordering. Maybe she'll close on Tuesdays, as well, now that she's pregnant. And I'm guessing she'll be hiring some help when the time comes. After the baby gets here, who knows?"

Brody couldn't understand why his indomitable and outspoken grandmother wasn't putting the screws on him to make an honest woman out of Cate.

"I told her we need to get married," he said, wincing inwardly at the defensive note in his voice.

Isobel rolled her eyes. "Ye can't club the lass over the head with a broadsword and expect her to do yer bidding. Cate has a mind of her own, boy. Things were different in my day. But this is the modern era. She doesn't need you to *save* her."

Nausea swirled in his belly. Deep inside, he'd been counting on his grandmother to swing the vote his way. "I see," he said slowly. "Then tell me why I'm not on the plane with Duncan right now."

His grandmother limped over and kissed the top of his head. "Ye're the only one who can answer that question, my lad. And ye'd better get it right, because if you hurt my lovely Cate, I'll have your head on a platter, grandson or no grandson."

Cate stood in the middle of her small bedroom and surveyed the piles of clothing strewn across the bed. Packing to move up to Miss Izzy's house had seemed like a simple chore until she realized that very few of her clothes would be suitable for pregnancy.

One or two unstructured dresses. A few loose tops. A skirt with an elastic waistband. None of her pants. It seemed her first chore would be to go online and order the basics of a new wardrobe.

She was finding it harder and harder to concentrate. Fortunately, today was Sunday. She had the whole day ahead of her to organize her life and gather what she needed to relocate. Even now she had deep reservations. Not about helping Miss Izzy. That was a given. But putting herself more deeply into the bosom of the Stewart family could make things awkward when the baby came.

The child would carry Isobel's blood. Knowing how the old woman felt about her Scottish heritage meant this baby would be a symbol, a link to Geoffrey, a tangible reminder of all that Isobel had given up to become a bride in America.

Cate paused in front of the mirror over the dresser and pulled her soft ivory knit top flat across her belly. Her stomach definitely pooched out. Sometimes that new physical manifestation scared her. This morning, with the sun shining and the nausea temporarily at bay, her little baby bump made her smile.

Unlike her own childhood, this baby was going to be smothered in love. Boy or girl, it didn't matter. Having a little daughter to dress in soft fabrics and colors would be joyful and sweet. On the other hand, a tiny boy crafted in Brody's image would steal her heart just as quickly.

It was easier to imagine herself as the single parent of a daughter. After all, Cate knew what it felt like to have crushes and periods and acne and friends who did stupid things. But boys? That was another worry entirely.

Even so, raising a male infant and toddler and young boy would be doable, surely. It was the future that gave her nightmares. When Cate's teenage son or daughter grew old enough to make his or her own decisions. Like defiantly hopping on a plane for Scotland and choosing to live with the father they had never known.

How would she explain that Brody had not wanted children? That this conception, like Cate's own, was an accident.

Her parents had done the right thing. They hadn't abandoned their daughter. Nor had they distanced themselves physically. It was the intangibles she had missed out on. Things like affection and humor and genuine familial bonds. Those gaps had left emotional scars. As a child, she filled the void with books and reading and an active imagination. Later in life, when she was finally out on her own, she continued to look for something she had never known, but in that instance, the consequences were tragic and painful.

In the midst of her soul-searching, the bell at the top of the stairs tinkled. It was linked to the front door of the bookshop, which meant she had a visitor. When she peeked out the front window, her breath whooshed out of her lungs and fogged the glass. Although the angle was such that she couldn't see the person who stood at her door, the vehicle parked at the curb was Brody's rental car.

With her heart pounding wretchedly fast, she glanced in the mirror again and groaned. She hadn't been expecting anyone to drop by. She'd barely even brushed her hair, and a little lip gloss would have been nice.

Now she didn't have time for such simple luxuries. The bell rang again. She could almost *hear* Brody's impatience in the rapid dinging.

All the way down the steps, she gave herself a lecture. No kissing. No arguing. And definitely, no physical contact of any kind.

When she turned the bolt and pulled open the door, Brody swept in like a conquering hero. He scooped her up and kissed her on the forehead before setting her on her feet. "Granny sent me to help you pack," he said. "Show me where the boxes are, and we'll get started."

Cate counted to ten slowly, telling herself that one platonic kiss couldn't derail her determination. "I could definitely use help moving boxes later today, but for now, I have things under control."

They were both being so polite it was almost comical. Was Brody thinking the same thing she was? That the shop was closed and she had a very comfy and cozy bed just up the stairs?

He frowned. "I'm here. I know how to pack clothes."

She folded her arms across her chest. "Why aren't

you on a plane with your brother?" She refused to let him know she was desperately glad to see him.

"Do we have to stand here for this conversation?"

"Fine," she said. The stairwell was narrow. Was he looking at her butt as they climbed the steps? Flustered and embarrassed at the mess she had created, she waved him to a chair at her tiny kitchen table. "Sit, Brody."

He cooperated, but the look in his eyes told her he was only biding his time.

She opened the fridge. "You want a beer?"

"No. I'm here to help you move."

"I don't need help *packing*. I've already told you that. Come back after dinner."

"Nope. Granny says you're in a fragile state. She doesn't want you exerting yourself."

"And what do *you* think, Brody?" Ah, hell. She was flirting again. Anytime she was around the handsome Scotsman, it seemed as natural as breathing. She handed him a Coke and opened one for herself, joining him at the table.

"Aren't you supposed to give up caffeine?" he said.

"Stop it. Right now. I refuse to take pregnancy advice from a man who has probably never even changed a baby's diaper."

He lifted an eyebrow. "Have you?"

"No. but that's beside the point. Seriously, Brody. You'll be in the way right now. I think I can load a few boxes without fainting."

He popped the tab on his soft drink and took a swallow. When he set the can on the table, his lips quirked. "Sorry, Cate. I can't go back up the mountain without you."

She pointed a finger. "You're scared of your grand-mother."

"Damned straight. Besides, I thought you and I could make plans for the wedding while I help you pack."

His bland smile infuriated her. "There's no wed-ding...nothing to plan. This baby is mine. This preg-nancy is mine. You're off the hook. If Miss Izzy is pressuring you, I'll talk to her."

Brody got a funny look on his face.

"What?" she demanded.

"Actually, Granny told me not to press the marriage thing."

Cate swallowed, refusing to admit her feelings were hurt. Did the tiny Scotswoman think Cate wasn't good enough for her grandson? "I see." She took a quick breath. "It's just as well. I told you it was a bad idea."

Brody leaned forward, elbows on the table, his gaze direct and intent. "You can trust me, Cate. I would never cheat on you, I swear. And our kid will have every ad-vantage."

"I'm not interested in your money, Brody."

"Money isn't evil."

"Maybe not. But it's not a substitute for love. You said it yourself. You don't want to settle down. It's okay. Really it is."

"Damn it, Cate." He jumped to his feet and paced, all evidence of the relaxed Brody wiped away in an in-stant. "You have to understand. My parents divorced when Duncan and I were children."

"I know. Isobel told me. And I'm sorry. But that's all the more reason not to jump into marriage."

"That's what I thought, too. Up until now. I felt like such a stupid clueless kid when they split up. I thought they were pretty cool parents, actually. I never heard them arguing or fighting. At least not until they decided they were done. After that things got bad fast. That's when Duncan and I came to the States and spent a few months with Grandda and Granny."

"You were lucky to have them."

"More than you know. What I'm trying to say is that I spouted off some stupid stuff to you. But I want to retract that self-righteous speech. I need a do-over. Please, Cate."

Her chest burned. "You and I wouldn't stand a chance."

"You don't know that." He paused behind her chair and stroked the back of her neck. "We have something powerful between us, Cate," he said quietly. "We could make it work."

She stood up to face him. The fact that she wanted so badly to say yes told her she had to fight. "I can't do this right now. You're pressuring me, and it's not fair."

"So you'll think about it?" His lopsided smile was disarming.

"If I say yes, will you leave me alone?"

He brushed the back of his hand over her cheek. "If you're expecting me to be honest, you won't like my answer."

"Forget it," she muttered.

He caught a flyaway strand of her hair and rubbed it between his fingers. "May I ask you a personal question?"

"I suppose…" But she tensed inwardly.

His shoulders hunched the tiniest bit as if he was uncomfortable. "Would it be weird if I touched your stomach? I'd like to feel it. The baby, I mean."

"Oh." She swallowed. "I don't think it's weird. You do remember I was half-naked with you last night?"

His chuckle sounded raspy. "I might have been a tad single-minded. Plus, you distracted me with your Amazonian breasts."

"Oh, please. They're not *that* big." She couldn't help giggling, and then was mortified.

"Made you laugh."

His satisfied masculine smile caught something deep in her heart and squeezed it hard. Being with Brody was like the first day of summer vacation. Everything seemed exciting and new, bursting with possibilities.

She bit her lip and told herself this tiny moment was no big deal. Lifting her shirt with one hand, she lowered the zipper on her old faded jeans. The pants hadn't been buttoned anyway. When she glanced up, Brody's cheeks were flushed and his eyes had a weird unfocused look to them.

"Go ahead," she said. "It's fine."

Slowly, he reached out and laid his large, warm palm flat on her swollen belly. Her navel and the surrounding real estate had never been particularly erogenous zones. But when Brody Stewart caressed the barely-there mound from the baby they had created together, her knees weakened, and she felt everything inside her melt.

She thought he might jerk his hand away. Seeing and touching the reality of conception was much different from a theoretical discussion about babies and marriage. Still, far from seeming squeamish about the pregnancy, Brody's gaze held wonder. "What does it feel like, Cate?"

"Odd. Wonderful. As if I have a secret, and I want to savor it." Did he even realize he was stroking her? Back and forth. Softly. Gently.

"Do you know if you want a boy or a girl?"

"I've thought about it, of course. I understand girls better than I do boys. The latter idea scares me, to be honest."

Having Brody touch her like this eroded all her high-minded notions of keeping distance between them. She should step away…break the connection. But how could she move when he was so obviously spellbound by the changes in her body?

Nine

Brody was flooded with all sorts of disconcerting emotions. He wanted to coddle Cate and at the same time, he was consumed with a throbbing, urgent desire that went way beyond simple physical lust. Her gently convex tummy fascinated him. She was carrying a brand-new life. How incredible…

Only when goose bumps covered her skin did he realize how long he had been touching her. It was a struggle, but he made himself break the connection. "Thank you," he said gruffly.

She flushed adorably, tugging down her shirt and fussing with the zipper on her jeans. "Of course."

"Does it make me an insensitive male if I say I'll enjoy watching you get bigger?"

Cate wrinkled her nose. "I think *fat* is the word you're looking for..."

Brody chuckled. "I won't win this argument. C'mon, lass. Let's get started on your packing. The sooner I get you up to Granny's house, the happier she'll be."

In the end, it took them barely an hour to fill three suitcases and seven boxes, but they still weren't done. When Cate insisted on unloading the entire small bookshelf beside her bed, he winced and scratched his head. "Ye own a bookstore, woman. And I happen to know you have an e-reader. Why in the devil are we taking all these?"

His grandmother's houseguest-to-be thrust out her jaw, her expression mulish and determined. "My books make me happy and comfortable. I didn't know there was a limit on how much I was allowed to bring with me."

He held up both hands in surrender. "No limit. My apologies. But don't blame me if this won't fit into the two cars."

Cate sat down on the bed and burst into tears.

"What did I say? Is this a hormone thing?" Dear Lord, he was out of his depth already.

His question only made things worse. With a sigh of resignation, he joined her on the mattress and put an arm around her, tugging her head onto his shoulder. "It's going to be okay, my sweet Catie girl. Don't cry."

Seeing the capable, unflappable woman dissolve into an emotional mess shook him to the core. How was he supposed to support her and help her if she wouldn't let him get close?

Intuitively, he kept his mouth shut and simply held

her. It pleased him that her hair was down. He stroked it absently, feeling the silken strands beneath his fingers. When Cate's sobs finally dwindled to sniffles, he reached for a box of tissues on her nightstand and handed it to her.

While she blew her nose, he studied her face...saw the smudges beneath her eyes. "You didn't sleep well last night, did you?" he asked.

Cate grabbed another tissue, her gaze wary and embarrassed. "How do you know that?"

"You get weepy when you're tired. I remember."

She bit her lower lip. "How can I sleep when my whole world is about to change?"

"I have a solution for that." He pulled back the comforter. "You need a nap, lass. It's Sunday. We've most of the packing done. When you wake up, I'll take you out for lunch or we'll order pizza."

"I'm not a child," she huffed. But she scooted underneath the covers and yawned.

Brody smoothed the sheets and pulled everything up to her chin. "Do you mind if I stay here with you? I've had a few sleepless nights lately myself."

Her eyes narrowed in suspicion. "We're *not* having sex."

"No, ma'am. I understand. But turns out, there are other things a man and a woman can do in bed together. I'll even stay on top of the covers if that will make you happy."

"It would make me happy if you had gone back to Scotland," she grumbled. But her protest was half-hearted at best.

Brody kicked off his shoes and stretched out with a sigh. The brief hint of spring had come and gone quickly. It was cold again. And damp. Cate must have turned the heat down when she was working. Now the air in the apartment seemed frigid.

When he shivered involuntarily, Cate snorted. "Oh, for Pete's sake. Get under the blankets, you big ornery Scotsman. But if you lay a hand on me, I'll scream."

He hurried to take her up on the offer before she changed her mind. As he settled in beside her, his muscles and bones relaxed instinctively. *Ah, bliss.* Four months ago he had spent a lot of time in this very room, though little of it sleeping. Cate's bed was a wrought iron antique, painted white. The crisp cotton sheets carried a hint of lavender.

They were both lying on their backs. When he turned on his side to face her, her eyes were open, her head turned toward him. Green irises with flecks of gold were shadowed with thick lashes a shade darker than her hair. She had one arm extended over her head, her fingers grasping a curlicue in the headboard.

On one memorable occasion he had tied her wrists to that sturdy metal. He shuddered in remembrance.

Cate closed her eyes. "I'm so tired I can't see straight, Brody. Would you, could you, just hold me? Please…"

He dared to tease her. "What about that screaming thing?"

"Oh, shut up and spoon me."

"I thought you'd never ask."

She turned her back to him, and he scooted in close.

For a split second it was as if the world spun backward, and it was October, and he and Cate had just met.

He put his left arm around her and tucked it beneath her breasts, careful not to do anything that would get him kicked out. "Better?"

"Hmm…"

She was already half asleep. He listened to her steady breathing and kissed the nape of her neck softly. Holding her like this would cost him, but it was worth it. When Cate let down her guard, it was as if the past four months had never happened.

For a long time, he simply breathed in the scent of her. Where her bottom nestled in the cradle of his pelvis, his sex responded painfully. Everything about Cate was perfect for him. The warm, responsive, feminine body. Her sharp wit. A deep compassion for his crotchety granny.

He didn't know which was the right thing to do anymore. Didn't this baby deserve a father? Granny seemed to think that pressuring Cate into marriage was wrong. It wasn't what Brody thought he wanted. Even Cate seemed reluctant. Yet if he went home, he was almost positive the window of opportunity to secure her trust would be gone forever.

He closed his eyes and exhaled, feeling the air from deep in his chest escape. If he were at home on the Isle of Skye, he'd be out on the water by now. Boats were the place where he could think. Candlewick was a quaint, charming town, much like a small Scottish village in many ways. But it was landlocked, and Brody felt bereft.

He must have dozed. His body was comfortable, even while his brain wrestled with weighty matters. Dreams wrapped him in spiderwebs of sensation. Struggling, confused, he pursued something always out of reach.

When he finally surfaced, Cate was sprawled half on top of him, one of her legs trapping his. She was still asleep.

He blinked and strained to see his watch. It was almost one thirty, which explained why his stomach was growling. "Catie," he whispered. If she slept too long, she'd be awake again tonight. "Catie girl. Wake up."

"Mmph." She buried her face in his neck. "Don't wanna," she muttered.

He grinned, palming her bottom and squeezing. "Fair warning, lass. If you stay on top of me much longer, something is going to happen, promise or no promise."

One eye opened. Apparently, she hadn't grasped the compromising nature of her current position. "Did you try to start something with me asleep?"

"Hey," he said, genuinely indignant. "You're the one who moved, not me. Now either go back to your own pillow, or—"

She put a hand over his mouth, her grin mischievous. "Or what?"

His little Cate was feeling amorous after her nap, but he couldn't afford another misstep on his part. He removed her hand. "You said *no sex*," he pointed out calmly, although he had an erection that could hammer steel.

"We've both said things we regret," she said, her tone

airy and teasing. "Situations change." She nipped his bottom lip with sharp teeth and then kissed him lazily.

He swallowed hard. "You're not playing fair, lass."

"Make me forget, Brody," she whispered. "Turn back the clock. I liked being crazy and impetuous with you."

Something about that last bit bothered him. Was he Cate's walk on the wild side? "We need to talk," he said, trying to ignore the way her breasts thrust against the soft cotton knit of her top.

She unfastened the top three buttons of his shirt and licked his collarbone. "Later, Brody. Later."

A man could only withstand so much provocation. "Ah, hell." He gave in, because to resist her would be insane on multiple levels. Jerking her top over her head and tossing it aside, he sighed with pleasure at the sight of her voluptuous breasts spilling out of her standard-issue white bra. "Being pregnant suits you, lass. Ye're a feast for the eyes."

They attacked each other, ripping at buttons and zippers and laughing as they rolled over and over in the bed. "Don't let me fall," she said, the words husky and low.

"Never, Catie girl. Never."

He moved over her and into her and sucked in a startled breath at the tight fit. Despite last night's insanity at the restaurant gardens, he felt as if he hadn't had her in days. Greedy and hungry, he thrust to the hilt, pressing the mouth of her womb. Cate's low groan urged him on.

Cate whimpered when Brody pistoned his hips wildly. What had started as lazy afternoon sex quickly escalated. Sharing this bed with him was at once familiar and new. She carried his child. He wanted her to marry him.

Wrapping her legs around his waist, she canted her hips, begging him wordlessly for more and then more. Her body was like a stranger to her. Nerve endings and sensations sprang to life, carrying her along on a tide of wanting so intense, she felt as if she literally might die if he stopped.

Though the room had been cold before, they were both damp with sweat. Brody was still half dressed, one leg of his jeans down around his ankle. Her bra was trapped somewhere, the strap digging into her arm. Nothing mattered. "Brody," she gasped. "Brody…"

His chest heaved with the force of his ragged breaths. Her orgasm bore down on her like a wild, runaway horse straining for freedom. She wanted to feel it all, every incandescent second, but she shattered in his arms, crying out his name again and shuddering endlessly as her body found blissful release.

Brody cursed and went rigid, filling her with his life force. Then he collapsed on top of her and moaned into her tangled hair.

Long seconds passed as they struggled for oxygen.

He stirred at last. "Holy God." It was more prayer than profanity.

"I always heard that some pregnant women were insatiable when pregnant. Never thought it would be me."

She expected him to laugh. Brody always found a way to make her smile. But for once he was oddly silent. When he eventually levered himself off her and started pulling on his clothes, her stomach growled loudly.

Brody stood and tucked his shirt into his pants. "How 'bout I grab us a pizza?"

She nodded, abashed at his odd mood. "That sounds good."

"Back in a few." He scooped up the key to the street entrance and tucked it in his pocket.

When the door at the top of the stairs closed behind him, she grimaced. Brody was right. They needed to talk. But first, she had to finish the job they had started. Fortunately, the upstairs apartment was small. It didn't take long to eyeball closets and drawers and make sure she hadn't forgotten anything. Who knew if it would be six months or six weeks before she returned to this familiar nest? She and Miss Izzy might not get along on a daily basis.

Because her parents had structured almost every aspect of her life growing up, uncertainty was a hard thing to accept. Not only was she pregnant, but she had also agreed to look after a woman who might live forever or might keel over tomorrow. Cate was no nurse, but she was happy to keep an eye on Brody and Duncan's grandmother if it would give the family a feeling of security.

Brody returned in just under forty-five minutes bearing a box that smelled like heaven. Since she had cleaned up the kitchen already in preparation for leaving, she opted for paper plates and plastic cups.

They ate in an awkward silence that only increased in intensity as the minutes ticked by. Brody finished off his fourth piece to her two and drummed his hands on the table. "Tell me something, Cate."

The bite of pizza stuck in her throat. "Okay."

His mood was hard to pin down, somewhere between challenge and grumpiness, which was mighty strange for a man who had just had what Cate thought was the best sex of their relationship to date.

Since she couldn't read him, she allowed the silence to build. Let him take the conversational lead.

Finally, he leaned his chair back on two legs in a familiar pose. "A while back I asked Granny to tell me why you came to Candlewick five years ago. She said if I wanted to know, I'd have to ask you myself."

"I see." Her heart sank.

"So I'm asking." His beautiful cerulean eyes were stormy. His hands clenched in fists on the table.

The story didn't paint her in a flattering light. Maybe if she admitted the truth he would finally understand that marriage was out of the question. Where to start? After a pause to gather her thoughts, she shrugged. "You remember I told you that my parents were killed in a car accident?"

"Yes."

"It happened just as I started my first year of med school in southern California."

His brows flew to his hairline. "You're a doctor?"

"Not even close. I didn't make it until Christmas, unfortunately."

"What happened?"

"I fell in love."

He went pale beneath his tan. "Oh? With another student?"

"No. One of my professors. He was young, charismatic. I'd been traumatized by my parents' deaths. I was so damned lonely and vulnerable. It makes me sick to think about it. I was hungry for someone to care about me, Brody. How pathetic is that?"

He recovered some of his composure. "Makes sense, I suppose. You've told me your childhood left emotional wounds. With the tragedy on top of that, and you heading into a new environment… I guess I'm not surprised it was a hard time."

"He was married, Brody. A wife and two kids on the other side of town. Nobody knew. Certainly not me."

"Hell, Cate." He looked genuinely ill.

"The affair had been going on from the end of September until almost Thanksgiving break. Then one day it all came crashing down. The wife showed up on campus. Pitched a huge screaming fit. The board demanded his immediate resignation. And I was just the poor stupid woman who had fallen for his lies. Gullible. Pitiful. I packed up my tiny apartment, loaded my car and never looked back."

"Why Candlewick?"

"I did a real estate search for places as far away from the Pacific Ocean as I could imagine. Found the bookstore for sale. I had the life insurance money from my parents. This was the place I ran to…and meeting Miss Izzy was a bonus."

"I don't know what to say." Some of his pallor lingered. She shrugged, feeling twinges even now of shame and self-loathing. "You don't have to say anything. The fact is, I'm a lousy judge of relationships. I won't marry you, Brody. I thought I had found the love of my life, and it turned out to be a gigantic lie. I can't go through that again. I like being on my own. It's safer that way."

Ten

Brody had never been more confused. Cate was having his baby. That gave him a moral imperative to try to create a family. Didn't it? But he could hardly expect her to follow him to Scotland, not when she had baldly confessed that trust was hard for her.

As for Candlewick? There was nothing for him here, not one damned body of water bigger than a fish pond. Back in the Highlands he owned a whole fleet of boats, everything from sleek sailing vessels to tourist charters to workaday fishing trawlers. Water was his life. His ancestors had carved an existence from the icy waters of lochs and oceans.

The only alternative he could see was to work alongside his grandmother and try to help her as best he could. The prospect of never returning home to Scot-

We are prepared to **REWARD** you with 2 FREE books and 2 FREE gifts for completing our MINI SURVEY!

FREE
Value Over
$20!

You'll get...

TWO FREE BOOKS & TWO FREE GIFTS

just for participating in our Mini Survey!

Dear Reader,

IT'S A FACT: if you answer 4 quick questions, we'll send you 4 FREE REWARDS!

I'm not kidding you. As a leading publisher of women's fiction, we value your opinions… and your time. That's why we are prepared to **reward** you handsomely for completing our mini-survey. In fact, we have 4 Free Rewards for you, including 2 free books and 2 free gifts.

As you may have guessed, that's why our mini-survey is called **"4 for 4".** Answer 4 questions and get 4 Free Rewards. It's that simple!

Thank you for participating in our survey,

Pam Powers

www.ReaderService.com

To get your 4 FREE REWARDS:
Complete the survey below and return the insert today to receive 2 FREE BOOKS and 2 FREE GIFTS guaranteed!

▶ DETACH AND MAIL CARD TODAY! ▶

1 Is reading one of your favorite hobbies?

☐ YES ☐ NO

2 Do you prefer to read instead of watch TV?

☐ YES ☐ NO

3 Do you read newspapers and magazines?

☐ YES ☐ NO

4 Do you enjoy trying new book series with FREE BOOKS?

☐ YES ☐ NO

YES! I have completed the above Mini-Survey. Please send me my 4 FREE REWARDS (worth over $20 retail). I understand that I am under no obligation to buy anything, as explained on the back of this card.

225/326 HDL GMYG

FIRST NAME	LAST NAME

ADDRESS

APT.#	CITY

STATE/PROV.	ZIP/POSTAL CODE

Offer limited to one per household and not applicable to series that subscriber is currently receiving. **Your Privacy**—The Reader Service is committed to protecting your privacy. Our Privacy Policy is available online at www.ReaderService.com or upon request from the Reader Service. We make a portion of our mailing list available to reputable third parties that offer products we believe may interest you. If you prefer that we not exchange your name with third parties, or if you wish to clarify or modify your communication preferences, please visit us at www.ReaderService.com/consumerschoice or write to us at Reader Service Preference Service, P.O. Box 9062, Buffalo, NY 14240-9062. Include your complete name and address. HD-218-MS17

© 2017 HARLEQUIN ENTERPRISES LIMITED ® and ™ are trademarks owned and used by the trademark owner and/or its licensee. Printed in the U.S.A.

READER SERVICE—Here's how it works:

Accepting your 2 free Harlequin Desire® books and 2 free gifts (gifts valued at approximately $10.00 retail) places you under no obligation to buy anything. You may keep the books and gifts and return the shipping statement marked "cancel." If you do not cancel, about a month later we'll send you 6 additional books and bill you just $4.55 each in the U.S. or $5.24 each in Canada. That is a savings of at least 13% off the cover price. It's quite a bargain! Shipping and handling is just 50¢ per book in the U.S. and 75¢ per book in Canada*. You may cancel at any time, but if you choose to continue, every month we'll send you 6 more books, which you may either purchase at the discount price plus shipping and handling or return to us and cancel your subscription. *Terms and prices subject to change without notice. Prices do not include applicable taxes. Sales tax applicable in N.Y. Canadian residents will be charged applicable taxes. Offer not valid in Quebec. Books received may not be as shown. All orders subject to approval. Credit or debit balances in a customer's account(s) may be offset by any other outstanding balance owed by or to the customer. Please allow 4 to 6 weeks for delivery. Offer available while quantities last.

► If offer card is missing write to: Reader Service, P.O. Box 1341, Buffalo, NY 14240-8531 or visit www.ReaderService.com ►

BUSINESS REPLY MAIL
FIRST-CLASS MAIL   PERMIT NO. 717   BUFFALO, NY

POSTAGE WILL BE PAID BY ADDRESSEE

READER SERVICE
PO BOX 1341
BUFFALO NY 14240-8571

NO POSTAGE
NECESSARY
IF MAILED
IN THE
UNITED STATES

land made him break out in a cold sweat. How had he let his life get so fucked up?

Unfortunately, the day deteriorated after Cate's confession. They loaded up both cars and locked the store, making it up the mountain to Isobel's home just before five. Unloading took another hour. Soon, Cate was ensconced in a luxurious bedroom just across the hall from Brody's. His grandmother's suite of rooms was at the far end of the corridor.

Was Isobel playing matchmaker? Surely not. She hadn't been enthusiastic when Brody admitted he had more or less proposed to Cate.

For the time being, Brody's grandmother had hired a young woman from the town to come in and prepare dinner each evening. The presence of another person in the house made it virtually impossible to carry on any kind of personal conversation during the meal.

After dessert, Cate pleaded fatigue and disappeared.

Brody shoved back from the table and ran both hands through his hair. "I don't know if I can stay here, Granny. Maybe I should rent a place of my own for a few weeks."

"What are you afraid of, Brody?"

He jerked back, mouth agape. "I'm not *afraid* of anything, damn it. You were the one who said I needed to give Cate some space."

"Don't curse at me, young man."

"Sorry, Granny." He felt his neck heat. "I can't figure her out. Women are impossible."

"I may be ancient, but I still remember what it was

like when your grandda and I were keeping company. I thought he was an arrogant American ass."

"Really?" Brody chuckled. "I didn't know that."

"Oh, aye. The upstart thought he could sweep me off my feet and shower me with presents. I sent him packing more than once."

"How did he finally win you over?"

"He loved me," she said, the words simple and direct. "When I understood that, everything was easy."

Brody changed the subject awkwardly and spent the remainder of the evening pretending everything was normal when it was anything but. This house was not an unfamiliar place. He'd visited many times over the years. Still, it wasn't *home*. Like a new shirt that didn't fit exactly right, somehow he knew that Candlewick and even his grandmother's beautiful and luxurious home were not where he was supposed to be.

Which brought him back to his original problem. What was he going to do about Cate?

He was still prowling the darkened hallways at midnight, unable to sleep, when he stumbled upon Cate raiding the refrigerator. She turned guiltily, her expression illuminated by the small appliance bulb, and tried to hide a piece of pie behind her back. "I thought everyone was asleep," she said.

"I'm not the food police." He kept his tone light. "Isn't this the one time in a woman's life when she's supposed to be able to eat anything she wants, guilt-free?" He rummaged in a drawer for a couple of forks. "Come sit. I'll join you if there's more." He hadn't been interested in dessert earlier…too much on his mind.

"There's plenty," Cate said. "I love this new cook. Butterscotch meringue pie. Haven't had anything like it since I was a child."

They sat at the small table elbow to elbow. Neither of them opted for the overhead light. Instead, a small decorative Tiffany lamp cast just enough glow for them to see their plates. At first, they ate in silence. The pie filling was smooth and creamy, and the topping was exactly right.

Brody came up with a dozen sentences in his head and cast them aside. There was too damn much at risk for him to alienate Cate. At last, he set his fork on his empty plate and reached out to take one of her hands in his. She jerked, startled, when he touched her, but she didn't pull away.

"Cate…"

"Yes, Brody?"

She was wearing thin flannel pajama pants and a peach thermal top that made her skin glow. With her hair down around her shoulders, she looked far too young to be anyone's mother.

He traced her knuckles. Her long, slender fingers were bare. "I know I said I wouldn't push, but I'm torn, lass. Having us both live under this roof, given the circumstances, seems artificial at best. I want you, and I think you want me, but I can't see us sneaking around like two teenagers. It's disrespectful to Granny. I love her too much."

"I completely agree."

"So how do we get past the fact that I ache for you, Cate? Am I the only one?"

She shook her head slowly. "No. I feel the same way."

"If you married me, we could share a bed and a life."

Her expression was pained, her eyes dark with misery. "If you count the days we've actually spent together, Brody, we've known each other less than a month."

"True." He rubbed the heel of his hand against his brow where a headache pounded. "I understand what you're saying. On the surface, the idea is ridiculous. But over the centuries, people have married for far less practical reasons. We *like* each other, Cate. And we have sexual chemistry in spades. We've created a baby who carries our DNA. Why can't we give it a chance?"

"My doctors are here, Brody. And my health insurance. What would you do every day?"

He shrugged. "I don't know. Help Granny with the business. Look after you."

"Why is this so important to you?"

If he could answer that, his gut wouldn't be in a knot. "Honestly?" he said. "I'm not entirely sure. But I can't imagine walking away from you and our child, nor going back to Scotland and pretending my life is the same as it's always been. It's *not* the same, Cate. It can't be."

"What would you do about your boat business?"

Was he winning? Did he sense a softening in her? Elation filled his veins, but he tamped down his compulsion to press for the outcome he wanted. "Duncan is my partner. He's been handling the financial side for some time. The man is a whiz with numbers. If I ask him, he'll keep things running while I'm gone."

"And then what?"

"Damn it, Cate. Can't we make it up as we go along?"

She wrapped her arms around her waist. "If I'm going to agree to this, it would have to be for a set period of time. Let's say a year. We draw up legal documents that outline all the eventualities. After twelve months, if you go back to Scotland, the baby stays with me."

He clenched his jaw so hard, his headache tripled. "You expect me to leave my bairn?"

"That's why this won't work, Brody. You think getting married will solve something."

"It's a start," he said sullenly.

Suddenly, she grinned at him. "Wouldn't it be easier to live in sin?"

"Is that some kinky American custom I don't know about?"

"Oh, shoot. I forget you're not from around here."

"Are you casting aspersions on my intelligence?"

"Not your intelligence, Brody. Just your knowledge of American idioms. Living in sin is the same as shacking up."

"Shacking up?"

"Is there an echo in here?"

"Say what you mean, Catie girl."

She leaned a hip against the kitchen table, looking tired but incredibly sexy. "I don't think abstinence is going to work for us. Miss Izzy is less of a traditionalist than you think. I'll talk to her about it if you want me to."

"No," he said forcefully. The thought of having his lover discuss their sex life with his ninety-two-year-old granny freaked him out. "So let me get this straight. You won't marry me, but you're willing to fool around with a chaperone just down the hall?"

"Not a chaperone, Brody. Besides, she doesn't hear a thing at night when she takes out her hearing aids."

He put his hands over his face. "I'm in hell."

"Don't be so dramatic. I'm the one whose body is going to morph into a giant whale."

"Quit fishing for compliments. You're gorgeous and sexy. I can't look at you without wanting you. That's not going to change just because you have a cute little pregnant belly."

"It won't be *little* for long," she muttered.

He lifted her hand and kissed her fingers, lingering over the caress until Cate squirmed. "Do ye think you can sleep now?"

Heavy-lidded eyes looked up at him. "Will you be there?"

He stood, drew her to her feet and curled an arm around her waist, urging her toward the hall. "Aye. But I don't ken how much sleepin' there'll be."

Three weeks passed in the blink of an eye. Cate felt as if she were living two separate lives. She followed her usual schedule at the bookstore Tuesdays through Saturdays. The work kept her mind occupied, and when shipments came in, the job was physically challenging, as well.

All the hustle and bustle was good because otherwise, she would have spent her time incessantly wondering if she was falling in love with Brody Stewart.

She experienced all the signs. Increased heart rate. Butterflies in her stomach when he walked into the room.

The same urgent desire that had catapulted her into a physical relationship with a near stranger now bound her to him infinitely more. She *liked* him, and that was dangerous.

On Sundays and Mondays, Cate spent quality time with Miss Izzy. The moment had come, in the old woman's estimation, to clean out her husband's personal effects. The task was heart-wrenching and poignant. Cate helped sort clothing, but Isobel had to make the final calls.

A few things were set aside for the grandsons. A pocket watch. A well-used shaving set with sterling silver handles. Most of the items—the bulk of them—went to a local charity.

Cate didn't know what Brody did all day every day, and she didn't ask. She assumed he and his grandmother were dealing with things at the company headquarters. Isobel thrived having her grandson nearby, and she relished having Cate under her roof, as well.

The mundane routine of Cate's daily activities was underscored with a breathless happiness. Brody came to her bed every night, but he always returned to his own room before dawn. It was doubtful they were fooling anyone. Still, Isobel didn't challenge them. Even the housekeeper who cleaned twice a week couldn't know for sure.

Cate and Brody's lovemaking was at times tender and sweet. Other nights he took her forcefully, as if trying to prove without words that they were a couple.

Cate told herself she was living on borrowed time. This *pretend* situation couldn't last. Perhaps it was the pregnancy that enabled her to ignore all the ramifications lurking just beyond the bend in the road.

The pleasant fiction of her self-indulgent days was rudely ripped apart one afternoon in March. She had closed the bookstore early—given the lack of customers—and rushed up the mountain, eager to spend the evening with the man who was becoming far more to her than just the father of her unborn child, or even the lover who warmed her bed at night.

Brody was insinuating his way into her heart. His generosity and caring made her feel more special than anyone ever had. The man was almost unfailingly positive. He coddled her and showered her with gifts and made her feel sexy and desirable, even as her body bloomed with the changes of pregnancy.

The day that became a turning point gave no sign of what was to come. The only thing she could later recall was the old maxim that eavesdroppers rarely heard good of themselves. When she hurried through the house to find Brody and show him the stack of books she had ordered for the baby, she stopped short, just outside the den, when she heard her name.

Miss Izzy's voice was unmistakable. "Tell me, Brody," she said. "Why is this marriage to Cate so important to you?"

Cate's heart clenched in her chest, terribly afraid to hear his answer.

Brody's reply was oddly weary. "I don't know,

Granny. Part of it is pride, I suppose. I don't want people thinking I got Cate pregnant and didn't do right by her."

"So it's about *you* and not the baby."

"Not *just* that," he said, definitely irritated by his grandmother's prodding. "I want to be listed on the birth certificate as the father. I want the kid to have my last name."

"And you don't think Cate will accommodate your wishes regardless of your circumstances?"

"Maybe. I suppose."

"Stewart men have always had a knack for thinking with something other than their brains."

"Granny!"

Cate could almost feel Brody's face flushing.

Isobel chuckled. "It's understandable. You've helped create a new life. But I have to ask you, dear boy. Do you love Cate?"

Where Cate stood, the pause seemed to last forever.

At last, Brody replied. "I think I *could* love her. We only met a few months ago, and I was gone for most of that. But when we're together…"

He trailed off.

Isobel didn't mince words. "You *want* her, Brody. And you feel possessive. But it's not enough. Once lust and desire transmute into something less urgent, you have to have more. To sustain a marriage, there has to be a foundation of some kind, something more than physical."

"Or I'll end up like Mom and Dad."

Isobel snorted audibly. "Your parents are both wonderful people—individually. Unfortunately, their relationship turned toxic, and you and Duncan became collateral damage."

"I don't want to fail at marriage."

Cate forced herself to enter the room, even though her stomach heaved and she felt like throwing up. "That's why we're not getting married." She gave Isobel as much of a glare as she could muster for her petite, elderly friend. "I appreciate your concern, Miss Izzy, but this is between Brody and me."

Brody's pupils had dilated as if he was alarmed or embarrassed or both. "I didn't say anything to Granny that I haven't said to you," he muttered.

Except to admit that you aren't in love with me. The raw truth hurt like hell. Only then did Cate realize she had been weaving painfully naive fantasies. She knew better than most that men used honeyed words and sex to get what they were after. Brody was far more honorable than the professor who had humiliated her, but at the end of the day, he wanted certain things, and he was willing to try everything in his power to sway her to his way of thinking.

"I'm not angry, Brody." She kept her voice completely even. Calm. All the while, her heart shattered into a million painful fragments. She turned back to Miss Izzy. "If Brody and I were ever to get married—and that's a big if—it would be for practical reasons, and it would be temporary only. We would have a lot of details to work out before that time comes."

Isobel sniffed. "In my day we'd say you put the cart before the horse, sweet, stubborn Cate."

Brody put his arm around Cate. "This is *our* problem, Granny. You'll have to trust us to deal with it in our own way and in our own time."

Cate stiffened when Brody touched her. She couldn't bear his nearness. Not right now. And his words poured salt in the wound that was her bruised and aching heart. She jerked free and wrapped her arms around her waist. Her voice wobbled despite her best efforts. "I don't consider this child a *problem*, Brody Stewart. I'm sorry that you do. If you'll excuse me, I think I'll skip dinner and have an early night. I'll see you both in the morning."

Eleven

A man knew when he had been summarily dismissed. *Hell.*

Isobel's worried expression underscored his own unease. She shook her head. "I'm sorry, lad. Do you think she heard the whole conversation? I shouldn't have butted in."

Given his grandmother's obvious distress, Brody didn't have it in him to chastise her. "Not to worry," he said lightly. "I'll smooth things out with Cate."

"Not tonight."

"No," he said ruefully. "It won't be tonight."

Only when he undressed at 1 a.m. and crawled naked into his lonely bed did he realize how much he had come to anticipate the sweet hours with Cate at the end of each day. Her changing body was a miracle to him.

The wounded look he had seen in her eyes earlier troubled him. Was he at fault in this situation? He'd proposed marriage, damn it. What more could she expect from him?

A restless sleep did nothing for his disposition. He spent the long hours alternating between unsettling dreams and awakening to find himself with a painful erection. By the time he arrived in the kitchen the following morning, he was in a foul mood. It didn't help that Cate barely acknowledged his presence. Isobel had not made an appearance. One of the signs she was slowing down at all was that she liked to sleep in until nine or ten.

Brody poured himself coffee. The American custom was one he had embraced eagerly. Today he would have mainlined the caffeine if he could. Instead, he downed the first cup and started in on a second.

Cate sat at the small table in the breakfast nook, her head buried in a pregnancy magazine.

He took the chair at the opposite side of the table and stared at her, hoping to force a confrontation. Apparently, her ability to ignore him was greater than his patience for being ignored. "Look at me, Cate," he said, forcing the words between clenched teeth.

She glanced up, wrinkled her nose dismissively and returned to her reading.

Brody counted to ten. "I don't understand why you're so pissed at me," he said, aggrieved and truculent.

Very slowly, she folded down the corner of the page she had been reading, closed the magazine deliberately and met his ill humor with a bland green-eyed gaze.

"You called our baby a *problem*," she said. "I wasn't aware that my child and I were such a great hindrance to your welfare. I *would* tell you to get the hell on a plane and head back to your precious moors, but you're not a man known for taking direction well, now, are you?"

Her snotty tone sent him into the red zone. "You don't want to mess with me this morning, Cate," he said, each word distinct and as threatening as he could make them.

His attempt at cowing her bounced off as if she had sealed her emotions in a deep freeze. "Go away, Brody. Let me have my breakfast in peace."

This time he had to count to twenty. He was angry and horny and completely out of his depth. No woman he had ever known could yank him in so many directions at once. "Tell me what you want, damn it. I'm tired of guessing and coming up short."

Her chin shot up and fire flashed in her eyes. "I don't want *anything* from you. I thought I had made that abundantly clear. In fact, I don't care if I ever—" She stopped dead and hunched over the table, her expression equal parts stunned and startled.

"What is it?" he snapped. "What's wrong?"

She didn't reply. Her gaze focused somewhere on the far side of the room. Her body had frozen into complete stillness.

He jumped to his feet and put his hands on her shoulders, shaking her gently. "Talk to me, lass. Are you ill?"

Her head fell back against his chest and a tiny smile crept across her face. "I'm fine."

He stroked her cheek. "You're scaring me."

"It's the baby, Brody. I think I felt the baby."

He sat down hard in the nearest chair, loath to admit that his knees were wobbly. "Is that normal? Does it hurt?"

She bit her lip, still with that look of intense concentration. "Normal? Yes, I think. I'm almost five months. It's time. I'm not sure what it should feel like, but there was something…"

"May I?" He reached across the small space separating them, not waiting for permission. Reverently, he placed his hand on the rounded swell of her belly. "Where, Cate? Show me where."

"Here." She took his fingers and shifted them a few inches. "I don't know if you can feel it from the outside."

But he did. Distinctly, yet subtly. A delicate flutter that rippled beneath her skin and warmed his fingertips. "Good God." The baby had been ephemeral to him until this moment. A tiny, unspecified, barely-there idea.

His breath lodged in his chest and his eyes grew damp. The flutter stopped. He glanced up at her, alarmed. "Why can't I feel it now?"

Cate shrugged. "I don't know. Maybe she's sleepy."

"He," Brody said with certainty. "A Stewart male to carry on the line."

"Good grief." Cate rolled her eyes, but when she looked at him, her earlier antagonism had vanished, replaced by a sense of dawning wonder. He recognized it, because the very same feeling snaked through his veins, making him the slightest bit nauseated. Such wild, unfamiliar emotion was unsettling.

"I'm sorry about yesterday," he said, stroking her

hair from her face. "I hurt your feelings, but that wasn't my intention at all."

Some of her open joy faded away. She eluded his touch and stood, placing a hand on the table to steady herself as if her feet weren't on solid ground. "I'm sorry, too," she said, her expression sober. "I understand, I think. Or I'm trying to. I've been reading a lot, and everybody says men are at a disadvantage in the beginning, because the baby doesn't seem real."

Brody nodded slowly. "At the risk of sounding like a jerk, I'd say that's true. I've been more focused on you and how you're feeling."

"For me," Cate said, her eyes pleading with him to understand, "it's like everything I've known about myself is changing at once. My body. My emotions. My future. As scared as I was in the beginning, and as distraught, I never once thought about giving this child up for adoption. But that's on *me*, not on you. I won't let one crazy middle-of-the-night sexual encounter where I was fully participatory dictate the rest of your life. It's not fair to you, and it's not really fair to me."

"Why is it not fair to you, lass?"

She bit her bottom lip, her eyes shiny with tears. "Because I deserve to have someone by my side who is crazy in love with me. Maybe that won't ever happen. I don't know. But I do know that a lukewarm marriage of convenience and practicality sounds like a wretched, lifelong prison sentence."

Brody absorbed the hit without flinching. After knowing what Cate's parents had been like and then finally hearing the story of the man who had betrayed her trust and love by lying to her and humiliating her, he couldn't fault her logic.

Slowly, he nodded his head, his mind spinning. "I see what you're saying. I really do. But—"

She held up her hand. "Stop. Just stop. To you, this pregnancy is a problem, one you're trying so very hard to solve. I appreciate the fact that you're interested and that you care and that my welfare and the baby's are important to you. But I won't be any man's *problem*, Brody. I've spent my whole life being a problem for *somebody*. Now I'm on my own, and this baby is a miracle. I refuse to look at it any other way."

He swallowed the urge to argue and held up his hands. "Understood. Perhaps we could call a truce?"

Cate yawned suddenly, telling him that her night might have been equally as unsettled as his own. "Yes," she said simply. "I don't have the energy to do battle with you, Brody. But promise me you'll think about going back to Scotland. I'm very serious about that."

"Fine. I'll think about it." Still, no matter how much he missed his old life, he couldn't see himself walking away.

Cate struggled against an overwhelming tsunami of fatigue. She hadn't slept well without Brody in her bed. Admitting that weakness, even to herself, was alarming.

On top of her sleepless night, this latest confrontation had left her wiped out. "I'll see you tonight," she said, hoping to slip past him without incident. She needed to get to work.

He caught her arm as she walked by. "Thank you," he said gruffly.

They were so close she could inhale the masculine scent of his sleep-warmed skin. "For what?"

"Sharing that *first* with me. The baby moving. I'm glad you wanted our child, Cate. Pregnancy suits you."

She closed her eyes and allowed herself one brief moment to lean her head against his shoulder and absorb his strength. "You're a silver-tongued devil, Brody Stewart, but I'll take the compliment."

Stroking her hair, he chuckled. "Could you use any help at the bookstore today? Granny has decided not to go into work. She told me last night. The two managers are doing very well, and she wants them to know she trusts them. Actually, I was afraid the business would be in chaos with Grandda dying and Granny grieving, but things are solid."

"I'm glad." Cate sighed. Actually, she wanted nothing more than to climb back into bed. But the bookstore was her responsibility and her livelihood. "I'd love some company," she said. "Let me get a few things together and we'll leave in fifteen minutes... Does that work for you?"

He kissed her forehead and released her. "I'll have the car waiting."

Cate brushed her teeth and grabbed the large canvas tote that held the things she would need for the day. It was still packed from the afternoon before. On top were the handful of books she had been so excited to share with Brody. *Goodnight Moon. Pat the Bunny.* Two different Sandra Boynton board books. Already she was looking forward to snuggling with the baby at bedtime and singing silly songs as she rocked her son or daughter.

Wistfully, she removed the books from the tote and left them on the dresser. She had let herself get too far ahead on a road that went nowhere. There was a very good chance that Brody would not even be around for the birth. She still had four months to go.

Already, she struggled with the notion of where to set up a nursery. Did Brody and Duncan really want her to stay with Miss Izzy in the long-term? Cate was happy to keep her friend company, but Isobel's beautiful home was filled with priceless antiques and objets d'art. As soon as the baby started crawling and walking, the environment would become imminently unsuitable.

Cate was trying, really she was, to live in the moment and not to worry so much. With each day that passed, however, new questions arose.

Brody was as good as his word. When she stepped out the front door, he was waiting with the vehicle. But the car parked on the flagstone apron was not the nondescript rental sedan in which he and Duncan had first arrived. This beauty was a shiny, black, luxury SUV with tinted windows.

"What's this?" she asked, running an appreciative hand over the spotless hood.

Brody jingled the keys in his hand. "I bought it yesterday. Didn't make sense to keep the rental any longer since I'm going to be sticking around for a while."

"I see."

He opened the passenger-side door and helped her

in. As he did, new-car smell wafted out to mix with the crisp morning air. Cate breathed in the appealing scent and fastened her seat belt with a sigh of appreciation. The seats were high-end leather, buttery soft and oh-so-comfortable.

Brody chuckled and reached out to turn on the radio. "I'm glad you like it. I listed your name alongside mine on the contract. If and when I go back to Scotland, you and the baby will have a safe, reliable means of transportation. The crash-test ratings for this model are impeccable."

"Brody?"

"Hmm?" He glanced in the rearview mirror and pulled out onto the winding road that led to town.

"You're doing it again."

"Doing what?"

"Trying to take charge of my life. I'm a grown woman. I already have a car, a perfectly reliable means of transportation."

His frown was quick and unmistakable. "You do have a car," he said, "but it's a dozen years old, and besides, it's way too close to the ground. When you're eight or nine months pregnant you won't be able to get in and out. Not only that, this car is perfect for a car seat. You can put the baby in and out without having to bend over and break your back."

"And I suppose you've already bought the car seat, as well?"

"No," he said. "I assumed you'd want to choose that for yourself."

Blatant sarcasm wasn't satisfactory at all when the

object of her retort was too impossibly arrogant to realize she was making a dig at his expense. *She* kept drawing a line in the sand, and Brody continued to step right over it. If she wasn't careful, he'd end up in the delivery room helping some poor doctor deliver the baby.

Luckily for Brody, Cate was far too tired to put up a fuss about the car. She closed her eyes and catnapped during the quick trip into town. It was nice having someone looking after her. If she allowed it, Brody would wrap her in cotton wool and protect her from every difficult situation and challenging decision.

Unfortunately, she was going to have to develop a backbone very soon. Otherwise, the alpha-male Scotsman was going to take over her life entirely.

When they parked in front of the bookstore, all the businesses up and down Main Street were beginning to open for the day. The bank. The dry cleaners. The corner diner. An assortment of retail shops offering everything from clothing to candy. A handful of professional offices that accommodated lawyers and title companies and an acupuncture therapist.

Cate loved Candlewick's small-town ambience and relished the knowledge that her business was an integral part of the community. If she hadn't gotten pregnant, her life would have ticked along year after year with very little variation along the way.

This town and its residents had welcomed her when she arrived broken and alone. Izzy, in particular, had taken her under her wing. The old woman had seen Cate's lost soul and had coaxed Cate into wholeness and healing with homemade bread and cups of coffee and long, wonderful conversations about books and authors and whether or not the digital age was going to ruin intellectual curiosity.

While Cate was lollygagging and lost in thought, Brody had exited the driver's side and come around to open her door. "C'mon, woman. It's getting late."

His intervention startled her. She recovered quickly and hopped out of the car. Once she had unlocked the bookstore door and turned off the alarm, she turned to Brody. "Make yourself at home. Browse the shelves. I have a couple of things to do straightaway, and then I'll see if I can find a project for you."

He grinned, his eyes this morning the blue of a springtime sky. "Don't *invent* jobs for me, lass. I'm quite content to hang out and watch you work."

She left him in the New Fiction section, still laughing.

Her small office was tucked away in a corner at the back of the building. The antique rolltop desk that was her pride and joy always seemed to be stacked with catalogs and bills and advance reading copies. She had thought more than once about hiring help, but it had taken several years before she finally began showing a profit. Not only that, Cate was a very private person. It couldn't be just anyone she brought into her special spot.

This bookstore had saved her life. It was her home.

When the bell over the front door chimed a warning, Cate poked her head out of the office to see who it was. Brody was in the midst of greeting Sharma Reddick and her four-year-old twins.

Cate hurried out to meet them. "Hey, Sharma. I

haven't seen you in weeks." The young mother shopped often at Cate's bookstore.

Sharma grimaced. "The boys had the flu. We're only now rejoining the land of the living. They were driving me crazy, so I promised if they cleaned up every one of their toys, I would bring them down here." She turned to Brody. "Cate is a genius. She fixed up that little corner over there several years ago. Now it's the best spot in town for parents who want a few minutes of peace and sanity while they shop."

Brody grinned and eyed the two mischievous boys. They were happily playing on a six-by-six, brightly colored rug. Cate had added a small train table, a container of plastic building blocks, a tub of Matchbox cars and an old-fashioned school desk that opened up and held crayons and paper for budding artists.

"Impressive," he said.

Sharma beamed at him. "Do you have children, Mr. Stewart? I'm a single mom, so I'm always on the lookout for child-rearing tips."

Or fresh meat. Cate maintained her smile…barely. Sharma was a dear, but that didn't mean Cate wanted her panting after Brody. "Brody is Miss Izzy's grandson, Sharma. He's here visiting and helping with the cabin business."

"I see." Now Sharma's eyes held a new appreciation. Gorgeous *and* rich? What woman could resist that?

Cate took Sharma's arm and steered her away from Brody. "Let me show you the new kindergarten level pre-readers. I think the boys would love them, and it wouldn't hurt to get them interested before school starts in the fall."

Fortunately, the ploy worked. Brody was able to go back to perusing the Biography section, and he was close enough to the kiddie corner to make sure the boys weren't doing anything dangerous.

Sharma picked out two books each for the brothers and headed for the cash register, plucking her credit card out of her pocket. "It's a good thing my parents love reading, too. Now that they know about Dog-Eared Pages, they send the kids checks every few weeks to buy more books."

"Works for me," Cate said cheerfully. When she finished ringing up the sale, she glanced across the counter and grimaced inwardly. It would take her half an hour to clean up the mess. But Sharma was a great customer, so the inconvenience was worth it.

Brody was keeping his distance. Once, when Sharma wasn't looking, he shot Cate a comical look over the tops of the nearest shelves. Cate grinned at him. Sharma's pool of eligible men in Candlewick was limited. It made sense that she would see Brody in a positive light.

The woman, who was only a few years older than Cate, gathered up her progenies and headed for the front door. "I'll be back soon," she promised. "Tell Miss Cate goodbye, boys."

Cate followed them, smiling, and then gasped as she stepped on something and her foot slid out from under her. She went down hard, landing on her right hip and banging her elbow on the floor.

Twelve

Brody's head snapped up when he heard Cate cry out. Sharma and her twins were not even out the door yet. Cate was sprawled on the floor.

"Oh, Cate," Sharma cried. "I am so sorry."

Apparently, a small toy had unwittingly brought about the accident. Brody's heart stopped. Cate had fainted several weeks ago, but this was far worse. Had she bruised her abdomen?

Heart in his throat, he crouched beside her. Cate struggled to sit up. "Wait a minute," he said gruffly. "I need to make sure nothing is broken. It was an awkward fall." He ran his hands along her arms and then her legs.

Sharma hovered, squawking and apologizing and generally getting on Brody's nerves. "I'm all the time stepping on little toys at home. *See*, boys. See what you've done to poor Miss Cate."

The twins appeared suitably chastened.

Brody managed a smile. "I think it's best if we close the store so I can take Cate to the doctor. Do you mind turning the sign on your way out?"

"Of course."

Sharma took her dismissal well. She shooed her kids out to the sidewalk, flipped the *open* sign to the opposite side, and closed the door behind her.

Brody sighed. "Good Lord." He picked up a tiny car. "Is this the culprit?"

Cate nodded. "It was my own fault. I didn't see it. I hit the floor so hard my teeth rattled."

She was trying to be funny, but Brody could see that she was hurting. "We need to get you checked out," he said firmly.

"My obstetrician's office is forty-five minutes away at the regional medical center. Honestly, Brody, I don't want to deal with that today. I'm fine, really. I'm sure I'll have some wicked bruises, but there's nothing the doctor can do for that."

"True. But you can't tell me you aren't worried about the baby."

She couldn't deny it. Those beautiful summer-grass eyes were dark with anxiety. "Of course I am," she muttered.

"Is there no doctor here in town who would see you?"

"Only a walk-in clinic. I've never met the people, but you don't need an appointment to get in."

"We'll start there, then." He bent and scooped her into his arms.

"I can walk, Brody," she protested.

"Humor me, lass."

He carried her out to the car and deposited her in the passenger seat. Then he made a quick jog back inside to retrieve her purse and lock up the store. He was gone, all in all, maybe four minutes.

When he returned, Cate had both hands on her belly.

"Are you hurting?"

She nodded. "Yes. But it's muscles and bones. I don't think the baby is in trouble. I can feel her moving around."

"Thank God." Relief made him light-headed.

The clinic was located on the outskirts of town in an area that was far less scenic than Main Street. The strip mall was home to a loan company, the clinic and a nail salon. Apparently, this was a busy time of day, because every parking spot was taken.

Before he could stop her, Cate had her hand on the door and was climbing out. "I can get in on my own, honestly."

"Damn it." He watched her walk gingerly inside. The stubborn woman was obviously in pain.

It took him three times around the block before he was able to find a legal parking space. He threw the car in Park, jumped out and hustled to the clinic. Though the storefront was uninspiring, the woman at the reception desk was friendly enough.

"Hello," she said. "May I help you?"

Brody scanned the mostly empty waiting room. "I need to go back with Cate Everett."

The woman eyed him with some suspicion. "Are you her husband?"

For a split second he thought about lying, but karma was a bitch, and he couldn't take any chances. "No."

"Family member?"

"No."

Her smile was kind, but her response firm. "I'm sorry. You'll have to wait out here."

Brody came close to losing it. He couldn't very well storm the castle, though. Cate had walked in under her own steam. Surely she wasn't in any real danger. Then again, what did these people know about babies?

His wait stretched from thirty minutes to an hour. Then half an hour more. He couldn't even text Cate because she had left her phone on the seat of the car. When he stood up to pace, the receptionist frowned, but didn't stop him. In the interim, a few patients came out and left. A handful more checked in. What in the hell was taking so long?

When Cate finally appeared, Brody had worked himself into a frenzy. Only by studying her face was he able to put his fears to rest. She looked tired, but normal.

Once she had taken care of the bill, Brody took her arm and walked her slowly outside and down the sidewalk to where he had parked the car. "I told Granny I was taking you out for dinner," he said.

"It's only three o'clock," Cate protested.

"But you missed lunch, and that's not good for a pregnant lady. If you feel like riding in the car, I thought we'd go over to Asheville. I haven't been there since I was a teenager. Grandda took Duncan and me to a concert once."

Cate nodded. "I'd like that."

"We need to talk, Cate, and as much as I love my grandmother, we don't need an audience."

They were in the car and on the way by now, so he couldn't look at Cate directly, but she nodded slowly. "Okay. But no talking now, please. All I want to do is take a nap." She leaned her seat back and kicked off her shoes.

"Of course." He tuned the radio to a soothing station and adjusted the air. "Do you need a snack on the way?"

"They gave me crackers and two bottles of water. I still have one in my purse."

His hands clenched the wheel. "What did they say? Are you sure we don't need to get you to a hospital?"

She bent her knees and curled up in an awkward position. "Very sure. The nurse called and made me an appointment with my ob-gyn tomorrow. As a precaution. But I'm fine. They poked and prodded and checked all my vitals a dozen times. I think it freaked them out that I was already bruising. That's normal for me, though. The curse of fair skin."

He reached out and took her hand in his. "You scared the hell out of me, lass. I heard the thud when you hit the floor."

"It wasn't a picnic for me, either, Brody. And poor Sharma…"

"Serves her right if she was upset. She should have taken the time to clean up after those wild boys."

"They're not bad kids," Cate protested. "Just very active."

"If you say so."

Cate didn't try to pull her hand away. He was glad. He and Duncan had grown up every bit as rambunctious as the two little monsters who had visited the bookstore earlier. The Stewart brothers had suffered through broken bones and stitches and countless thrashings from their father. Even in the worst of those situations, he never remembered fearing for his *own* safety.

But when it came to Cate… Damn. He couldn't bear the thought of anything happening to her.

She was asleep almost instantly. He'd checked the route with his GPS during the long wait at the clinic. Now all he had to do was follow the road and think.

Summer would be here before he could blink, and with it, the need to return to Skye. The bulk of his tourist business took place during June, July and August. It wasn't fair to expect Duncan to cover for him that long.

Could Brody go back to Scotland for a couple of months and then return for the birth? Would his absence during that time create a rift between him and Cate that could not be repaired? Already, he felt guilty for leaving her when they first met. It made no sense, not really.

Never at any moment had Cate expected him to stay. He'd been in Candlewick back in October for the express purpose of checking on his grandmother and reporting back to the family. He'd been entirely up front with Cate about that.

The two of them falling into bed had been a complication he never saw coming.

Now they were having a baby.

No matter how many times he parsed the information, he couldn't come up with any clear answers.

He hit the outskirts of Asheville at rush hour. Though the mountains encircled the town, it was still a city, after all. Everybody was in a hurry to get home after work.

Cate didn't wake up until he had to slam on the brakes to avoid rear-ending a delivery truck that stopped without warning. "Sorry," he muttered.

She rubbed her eyes. "Please tell me we're close. I'm starving, Brody."

He chuckled. "Almost there." He'd Googled restaurants and found one in the heart of town that promised romantic fine dining. Neither he nor Cate were dressed formally, but it was only five o'clock, so he was counting on the early hour to make their attire unexceptional.

The small dining room was actually part of a boutique hotel. The maître d' welcomed them cordially and led them to an alcove partially hidden behind flowering trees. The corner booth was constructed of high-backed, dark, carved wood and cushions covered in crimson damask.

"This is beautiful," Cate said, smiling as she took in the white linen tablecloth and the crystal, silver and china.

"I was hoping you would like it." He seated her and slid into the adjoining bench. The ninety-degree angle of the booth meant he was close enough to touch her, but he could look at her, as well. That tiny detail was helpful, because this was an important moment, and he needed to be able to gauge her mood.

Their waitress was attentive but not obtrusive.

Cate gave the woman a bashful grin. "Don't judge me for this order. I'm eating for two and I skipped lunch."

"Not a problem, honey. I had three kids of my own. You'd better let yourself be pampered now. It's all downhill from there."

Brody passed Cate the basket of hot yeast rolls as the server walked away. "I hope she was kidding."

"How would I know?"

"Are you scared, Cate?" It was a question that had been on his mind a lot in the past few days.

She spread butter on the fragrant bread and took a bite, her expression reflective. "Scared? No. Not really. More like anxious and overwhelmed and totally unprepared. I know I still have months to get ready, but I'm not entirely sure what *ready* means."

It worried Brody that she had no mother or older sister to help her. Miss Izzy wouldn't be much of an asset, either. His grandmother's single childbirth experience happened about a million years ago. Everything about having babies had changed since then.

Over a meal of chicken Madeira and spinach salad and angel hair pasta, Brody touched on impersonal topics. Politics. The summer schedule at the bookstore. Miss Izzy's upcoming health checkup. With the server constantly coming back and forth, there were too many interruptions to say what had to be said.

At last, the dinner was done. The only thing left was to consume the rich slices of salted caramel cheesecake. For this course, they were left in peace. It helped that the restaurant had become progressively more crowded.

Brody put down his fork and took a deep breath. "I have to go back to Scotland soon, Cate. But I want you to marry me before I leave. Not so I can control you," he said hastily, "but because I want to have legal rights to protect you and the child."

Her expression was impossible to read. With her gaze focused on her dessert, he couldn't even see her eyes. "Why, Brody?"

The question was blunt. Unadorned.

"You know the reason. I've explained half a dozen times."

"I don't know why you're so worried about *protecting* me. You didn't even bother to come back and sit with me at the clinic. I was worried and bored and where were you? Checking email? It's not my problem that you need a piece of paper to ease your conscience, Brody Stewart."

Emerald eyes blazed at him. Cate was furious…probably had been the entire time since they left Candlewick.

His own temper kicked in. "Really? This is my fault now? Good God, Cate. I was pacing the floor. But I'm nothing to you, at least not as far as the doctor's office was concerned. I *wanted* to be with you. Of course I did. They wouldn't let me go back to the exam room."

"Oh." She deflated visibly. "I didn't think of that."

"Why didn't you tell somebody to come out and get me?"

She gnawed her lip. "I didn't want to seem needy. I just assumed you were happy where you were."

He grimaced and sat back in his chair. Cate, wearing a soft cotton sweater that matched her eyes, looked as if she was about to cry.

"We're not handling this very well, are we?" he said.

"No." She shook her head and used the cloth napkin to wipe her eyes.

The waitress approached with their ticket, but Brody waved her off. "Marry me, Cate," he said quietly. "Please. We can take a quickie honeymoon and then be back here to set up the nursery before I go."

"Before you go to Scotland, you mean..." It wasn't a question. Cate recognized his responsibilities almost as well as he did.

"Yes. I'll be gone eight weeks, ten at the most. That will put me back in Candlewick in plenty of time for the birth."

"And after the baby comes?"

This was the part that tightened his throat and wrenched his stomach. "I don't know yet. You'll have to trust me to figure that out." It was asking a lot of a woman whose vulnerabilities had been built betrayal by betrayal.

Her face was pale, her expression set. "I don't want to be married in a church. Not when we both know this won't last."

The stubborn tilt of her chin threatened to ignite his temper again, but he forced himself to see beyond her truculence to the many ways she had been let down by the people in her life.

"If that's what you want. We can have a civil ceremony." Already, regret trickled through his veins. This wasn't how it was supposed to be. Cate deserved so much more.

"Swear to me you'll never try to take my baby away from me."

He said a word beneath his breath that he rarely used. Her lack of faith cut deep. "You have my word, Catie girl. You can trust me, I swear."

Thirteen

A week later Cate stood in front of the cheval mirror in her bedroom at Isobel's house and examined her reflection with dismay. Buying a wedding dress for a simple ceremony when a woman was almost six months pregnant was not an easy task. Particularly in a place like Candlewick.

Because Cate hadn't felt up to a shopping trip in the nearby county seat, she had resorted to a trio of purchases online and had the packages overnighted. Unfortunately, none of the gowns worked.

Cate had in mind something simple but elegant. The first one was frillier than it had appeared in the photograph. She hated it so much she didn't even try it on. The next dress draped tightly and showed her tummy far too much. This last one was the wrong shade of cream, making her look washed out.

She undressed and tried not to panic.

By the time she and Isobel had repacked the order and passed the box off to Brody with instructions on how to handle the shipping, Cate was exhausted and near tears again. She hated the weepy feeling.

Isobel urged her to sit. "All right, my sweet lass. Let's take another tack. Would ye perhaps be interested in seeing my wedding dress? It's old-fashioned, of course, but it's been in a cedar chest since the week I wore it, and 'tis in good condition. It might suit."

Cate sniffed. "I'd love to see it." Miss Izzy was tiny. This would never work. But she didn't want to hurt the old woman's feelings. "Of course I would."

She followed the Stewart matriarch down the hall to the large master suite. Isobel hadn't changed a thing since returning home as far as Cate could tell. Geoffrey's pipe still lay on the dresser.

The cedar chest sat at the end of the massive four-poster. Isobel raised the lid, bent and carefully lifted out a tissue-wrapped bundle. She carried it around to the side of the bed and laid it reverently on the mattress. Suddenly, she stopped and put her hands to her face. "Ah, heavens, lass. I'm sorry. I didn't think this would make me weep. I miss my Geoffrey."

Cate put an arm around her and sighed. "We're a pair, aren't we? You grieving and me hormonal. It's a wonder Brody hasn't run for the hills. Are you sure you're okay with him marrying me? I wouldn't do anything in the world to cause you more heartache."

Isobel leaned her head on Cate's shoulder and wiped her eyes with a dainty lace-edged handkerchief. "I think it's the right thing to do, Cate. Giving the bairn a legitimate birth. And as for you and Brody, well, time will tell."

The quavering words were hardly a ringing endorsement. But Isobel, like many of her countrymen, was practical and down-to-earth. She'd lived a long time and seen it all.

Cate stepped away and touched the tissue-wrapped bundle. "I don't think we should disturb the dress, Miss Izzy. I'm a lot taller than you are. And not as thin."

"Nonsense." Isobel straightened her spine. "The differences in our heights will make it tea length, which is perfectly acceptable for a courthouse wedding. And I wasn't always so scrawny. I started shrinkin' when I got old."

Cate couldn't help laughing. "If you're sure."

"Take it there in the bathroom and have a go at it. I have a notion ye'll be surprised."

Isobel's wedding gown was a dream, a romantic, exquisite vision of times gone by. Cate undressed, slipped it on and looked in the mirror.

From bodice to hem, the fit was perfect, thanks in most part to the timeless design. Heavy cream satin. Cut on the bias. Not a single pearl or bead or speck of lace. It was astonishingly perfect.

The wide, low-cut neckline showcased Cate's assets. The fabric was designed to cinch beneath the breasts and fall freely to the floor. The fact that the hem landed a couple of inches below her knees proved Miss Izzy's point. On Cate, the wedding gown was tea length.

The rich, lustrous material was soft to the touch. It slid over her rapidly increasing belly gently—by no means hiding her pregnancy—but instead, subtly emphasizing her condition. With one last glance in the mirror, Cate opened the bathroom door and stepped out.

Isobel's eyes brightened, and she exclaimed, "Ah, lass. Ye're a vision, 'tis true. Please tell me you like it. Lie if you have to. I've got my heart set on it now, you wearing my dress, that is."

Cate shook her head in bemusement. "Of *course* I like it," she said. "I feel like a princess."

"Don't move," Isobel said. She scurried across the room to the dresser. Lifting the lid on a large, carved wooden box, she examined the contents, then scooped something out.

She turned back to face Cate. Her hands were cupped together, hiding the prize. "Don't look, Cate. I've another surprise for ye. In fact, close your eyes. Don't peek until I give ye the word."

"Yes, ma'am." Cate stood in one spot obediently, not sure what Isobel had up her sleeve next. Moments later she felt the old woman's small, gnarled fingers brush the back of her neck.

"Geoffrey gave me these on the day we were wed," Isobel said. "The puir man nearly bankrupted himself, but he was determined his bride would have a suitable wedding gift." She steered Cate toward the mirror. "Ye can look now, lass."

Cate opened her eyes and gasped softly. "Oh, wow.

They're gorgeous, Miss Izzy." The strand of pearls was perhaps twenty inches long. It fell just at the tops of Cate's breasts. The color of the aging pearls matched the dress perfectly. Cate touched the creamy beads reverently. "I don't think I can wear them, though. I'd be terrified they might break. I do appreciate the thought."

Isobel got up in her face and shook a finger. "Don't talk back to yer elders, my girl. Brody's grandfather picked these out, and now Brody's bride will wear them."

"This isn't a real wedding, Miss Izzy. You know that. It seems disrespectful at the very least."

Isobel harrumphed. "Ye'll still be legally wed, no matter what nonsense you and my grandson have cooked up between you. History means something to we Scots, Cate." She touched Cate's baby softly. "This bairn inside you carries the blood of Highland clansmen. Strong. Honorable. Wed to the land they loved. And by the by, I can't believe you and Brody are being so stubborn. It's the twenty-first century. We should know by now if this wee one is a boy or a girl."

Cate grinned, still stroking the pearls warmed by her skin. "It's going to be a surprise. To all of us. Brody and I want it that way."

"Makes no sense to turn yer back on technology," Isobel muttered. Her criticism was not new. She was like a little child anticipating Christmas when it came to this baby.

Cate took one last look in the mirror and exhaled. "I suppose we're done here. The dress. The pearls. I already own a pair of ivory sandals that will work. Thank you for doing this, Miss Izzy. You saved me."

Brody stood in the foyer of his grandmother's elegant home and wrestled with the knot in his tie. Under other circumstances, he would be wearing his full dress kilt on his wedding day. Instead, he'd been forced to settle for a dark, hand-tailored suit. The uniform of the wealthy American male was perfectly acceptable, but Brody was Scots to his bones.

He should be wearing his kilt.

The two women in his life were supposed to have met him fifteen minutes ago. The delay stretched his nerves. His hands were clammy. His stomach churned.

When Cate appeared without fanfare from the hallway, his breath caught in his chest. "C-cate," he stuttered.

Her smile was tentative. "Hey, Brody. We're almost ready. Your grandmother forgot her hearing aids and went back to get them."

"Ah." He cleared his throat. "You look incredible, lass." Her hair fell like liquid gold in softly curving waves.

Cate smoothed her skirt self-consciously. "This is your grandmother's wedding dress. I couldn't find anything that would work, so she offered me her gown. It's not too much, is it?" Big green eyes stared at him.

He shook his head. "Not at all. You look like a Madonna." He wanted to say more, but she seemed as nervous as he felt, and he didn't want to venture into intimate territory when they weren't going to be alone.

Since Isobel arrived moments later, he was glad he had held his tongue.

Soon, they were on their way down the mountain. The county seat was thirty-five miles away. Isobel and Cate sat in the back of the car, leaving Brody alone with his thoughts. The old adage about it being bad luck for the groom to see the bride before the wedding wasn't really practical in this situation. There was no one to drive the females to the courthouse but Brody.

He had asked Cate in a roundabout way if there was someone she would like to have with her during the ceremony. She had said no. That worried him. Shouldn't Cate have at least one or two girlfriends to confide in? Isobel was a wonderful woman, but several decades separated her and Cate.

He glanced in the rearview and unexpectedly caught Cate staring at him. Her cheeks were flushed, her expression hard to read. Was she thinking about backing out of this wedding? The possibility made him antsy.

At the courthouse, their little trio elicited few stares. Despite the pregnant bride and her elderly attendant, Brody, Cate and Isobel were far from being the most unusual people waiting to be wed.

At last, it was their turn. Brody was so rattled it took him three tries to find the pocket where he had tucked Cate's wedding ring. Suddenly, the whole thing felt wrong.

Cate picked up on his unease. "Brody?" She scanned his face. "Are you sure this is what you want?"

"I didn't mean for it to be so clinical," he muttered. "We should at least have had a minister."

Cate lifted one beautiful shoulder and let it fall. "You needed legalities," she said quietly. "This will suffice."

Soon, the judge was speaking. Brody couldn't have repeated a single word or phrase of the ceremony afterward, even if he'd been faced with a firing squad. His whole brain went blank. All he could do was stare at his bride and mutter his responses at the appropriate places.

The only one that really registered was *with this ring, I thee wed.* He repeated the words and slipped the circle of platinum onto Cate's slender finger. Too late, he wished he had bought her an engagement ring, as well.

She curled her fingers into a fist and exhaled audibly. To his surprise, she had a ring for him, too. It was heavy and wide, the gold etched with a Gaelic pattern. When she took his hand in hers and pushed the ring against his knuckle, her touch made him shudder.

Suddenly, he wanted her. Intensely. Inappropriately, given the witnesses around them. Hoping that his jacket hid the state of his arousal, he helped her with the ring and kept her hand in his for the final words.

At last, it was over. Granny Isobel cried and hugged them both. Cate smiled, but she was pale, too pale.

Brody took Cate's shoulders in a gentle grasp and bent his head. "Happy wedding day, Mrs. Stewart." He kissed her long and deep, his heart slamming in his chest. Cate's lips clung to his. Her scent filled his lungs.

Slender arms came up around his neck, and she clung to him. "Aye, Mr. Stewart," she whispered. "I suppose it is."

He held her carefully, very aware of her baby bump. Isobel interrupted his concentration. "Tell her about the surprise, Brody," she said, her eyes twinkling with excitement. "Tell her."

Cate pulled away and smoothed her hair. "Surprise?"

Brody gave his grandmother the stink eye and waved her off. Escorting Cate to a corner of the room, he bent his head and kissed her temple, because he couldn't help himself. Touching her was an addiction. "Mrs. Tompkins is going to stay with Isobel for a few days. Granny packed your bags. They're in the back of the car. I've booked us a four-night honeymoon in Key West."

Far from being excited, his new bride frowned. "That's not necessary. You know this wedding isn't the real thing. A honeymoon would be inappropriate and over-the-top."

He held his temper with difficulty. "Make no mistake, Cate. We're married. *For real.* You are my wife, and I'm your husband." Saying the words aloud gave him an odd feeling.

"For now," she said, her expression both mulish and panicked.

His momentary anger faded as rapidly as it had come. Poor Cate looked overwhelmed. "Don't make a big deal about it," he said gently. "Everyone knows that life with a newborn is difficult and chaotic. If it makes you feel better, think of this as a pre-baby, relaxing getaway. You deserve to be pampered."

"I'm not sure I feel like flying in my condition."

"I've chartered a small, private jet. We'll be the only passengers. You'll have plenty of privacy and room to be comfortable."

"I suppose you've thought of everything." She bit her lower lip.

He took a gamble. "I won't make you go, Cate. I can cancel if that's what you want."

She reached for his lapel, adjusting the single white rosebud pinned there. Brody had bought her an enormous, expensive bouquet of matching roses with freesias and eucalypti. "I've never been to Key West."

"Neither have I. We can explore together."

"And share a bed?" Those cat eyes stared at him blandly.

"It *is* a honeymoon," he pointed out. "And it's our wedding day."

Sexual tension shimmered between them. For a moment he flashed on an image of him lifting her satiny skirt and taking her up against the wall. Sweat beaded his forehead. "Yes or no, Catie girl. What's it going to be?"

He saw the muscles in her throat work as she swallowed. This close to her, he could see the deep valley between her breasts.

"Take me to Key West, Brody. I want to be alone with you before you go back to Scotland."

Fourteen

Cate felt like a fairy-tale princess if one overlooked the fact that she was six months pregnant. Isobel had hugged her and cried as they left the courthouse. Both Brody *and* his grandmother had insisted that Cate continue to wear her wedding dress and carry her bouquet. There was no hiding the fact that she was a very unusual bride.

During the brief drive to the Asheville airport, Brody behaved himself. When he held her and kissed her after the ceremony, she had felt the evidence of his arousal. Knowing he still wanted her went a long way toward soothing her doubts. Perhaps Brody was right when he said that many couples began a life together with much less in common.

She had dreaded the usual airport ordeals, but her

fears were groundless. Apparently, Brody's money made a host of hurdles disappear. In no time at all, they boarded the sleek private jet and strapped themselves into large, comfy seats. Although there was no flight attendant, the small, luxurious plane was stocked with every conceivable amenity.

While the pilot and copilot ran through the preflight checklist, Brody offered Cate a flute of sparkling cider. "To my blushing bride," he said, touching his glass lightly to hers.

He was incredibly handsome in his tailored suit that fit his masculine, athletic frame perfectly.

Cate drank thirstily. It had been hot in the courthouse. She felt limp and rumpled. Because she had been too nervous to eat before the ceremony, now she was starving. "Are those sandwiches?" she asked, trying not to let Brody see how totally freaked out she was.

His grin was indulgent. "Aye." He opened the container and offered it to her. "We'll have a special dinner tonight, but this should hold us until then."

Cate was glad of the meal for more reasons than one. Eating gave her a way to ignore Brody to some extent. Only a narrow aisle separated their seats. The whole cabin was small, and Brody was a large man. His presence made her shaky. Or maybe she was getting airsick.

At this point in their relationship, her feelings for him were a weird mélange of excitement and dread.

Fortunately, by the time she finished eating, there was plenty to occupy her attention outside her small window. The pilot had flown south and east, and now their route hugged the coastline. She spotted miles of ocean sparkling far below.

Brody startled her when he touched her shoulder. "How are you feeling, Cate?"

She turned her head reluctantly. This man was her husband. *Her husband.* "Um, fine, I suppose."

His grin was lopsided. "Hardly a glowing affirmation on your wedding day." He caressed her elbow, his warm fingers sending gooseflesh down her spine and everywhere else.

Out of nowhere, stupid tears threatened again. "Stop it, Brody. Don't pretend. Playacting isn't necessary. I already feel like a fraud. You'll only make it worse."

His lighthearted smile was instantly replaced by a scowl. Blue eyes turned icy, and his jaw tightened. "Make no mistake, Catie girl. This marriage is real. Ye may not have had ten bridesmaids and a string quartet, but you *are* my wife. For better or worse." The utter determination in his gravelly voice sent a frisson of unease through her belly.

"And what if it's for worse? What then?" Despite her best efforts, tears spilled over and rolled down her cheeks.

Brody's expression hardened. He released her. "You know the options. We stay married for the bairn, or we get divorced."

"I don't know why you made us do this," she cried.

He stared at her, his expression glacial. "I never forced you, Cate. That's not fair."

She swallowed hard. He was entitled to his anger. Gripping the armrests, she sniffed and then wiped her face with the back of her hand. "I apologize. You're right, of course. It's been a difficult few weeks. At the risk of sounding like a cliché, these stupid pregnancy hormones are making me a little crazy."

He nodded, his gaze hooded. "Why don't you rest? I'll wake you up when we land."

The closer they came to Key West, the more Brody fumed and brooded. He had only himself to blame for this colossal mess. He'd pushed her too hard. And the hell of it was, he was not at all sure he had done the right thing. Not when it made Cate so skittish.

She had been more comfortable with him back in October when they barely knew each other.

Now those wary cat eyes constantly watched him. What was she thinking? How was he supposed to guess? She kept her emotions so damned guarded all the time. Why couldn't she relax and trust him? Was that so much to ask?

He studied her while she slept. Her hair was caught up today in a fancy concoction that was nothing more than a challenge to a hungry male. Already he imagined removing each pin until the entire mass of soft, silky waves tumbled into his hands.

When she rode him, that curtain of hair would fall across her full breasts. The image in his brain sent a signal to his groin, increasing his discomfort. In his gut, he believed that sex was the place they connected. Maybe if he kept Cate in bed for the next four days they would find enough common ground to survive this marriage.

She slept deeply, her head tilted to one side. It was

no wonder he had fallen instantly in lust with her last October. She was exquisite. Creamy skin. Classic features. Only now did he acknowledge the stubborn tilt to her chin. It should have been a tip-off.

Still, he would have pursued her regardless. Nothing short of a wedding ring or an outright no on her part could have dissuaded him from exploring the intense sexual attraction that had tormented him from the first moment he saw her.

A quiet ding interrupted his troubled thoughts. The copilot appeared in the doorway. "We'll be landing shortly, Mr. Stewart."

"Thank you."

When the man disappeared, Brody shook Cate's arm gently. "Wake up, Cate. We're almost there."

She surfaced slowly, her expression groggy. "That was fast."

"You were out for a long time."

"Sorry," she muttered, smoothing her skirt.

"I'm glad you rested," he said simply. "Stress is exhausting."

"And what about you?"

"I dozed a time or two."

"That's not what I meant. I want to know if all this has been stressful for you?"

"Of course it has," he said. "Look, Cate." He stopped, weighed his words and sighed. "I propose a truce. We could both use a holiday, right?"

She nodded. "Definitely."

"Then let's do that," he said. "We'll agree not to talk about the wedding or the marriage or the baby at all.

Just two people running away from home to have a little fun in the sun."

Cate held up her left hand, the one wearing his ring. "And I'm supposed to forget about this?"

He grimaced. "Take it off if you want to. I wouldn't expect you to be uncomfortable."

She leaned across the aisle and took his hand in hers. "I don't want to take it off, Brody," she said earnestly. "But I like your idea. No more squabbling until we're back in North Carolina. It's a deal."

The feel of her warm, slender fingers twined with his larger, rougher, masculine ones settled something in his gut. "You think we can go four whole days without fighting?" he teased.

At last, her smile was genuine, her eyes unclouded. "We'll give it our best shot."

After that, the afternoon improved. Their landing and deplaning in Key West was low-key and uneventful. Brody and Cate both were taken aback at how tiny the airport was. Even so, the car Brody had ordered was right outside, ready to whisk them away to their waterfront hotel.

There were no natural beaches in Key West. The island was built on the remnants of an ancient coral reef, rocky and remote. Still, who needed sand when brilliant blue waters and tropical breezes made the island a haven for artists and musicians and writers and tourists like Cate and Brody.

Despite Brody and Cate's détente in regard to the wedding, the hotel was prepared to give them the full bridal experience. It was too late for Brody to wave off the fanfare, so he stood by in silence, groaning inwardly as the manager greeted them effusively and insisted on procuring a crystal vase for Cate's bouquet.

Finally, the flurry of hotel employees departed, leaving the newlyweds alone in what was by any description an incredible suite. Cate threw open the double French doors and exclaimed. "Oh, Brody, this is amazing."

The air was warm and soft and fragrant with the scent of bougainvillea. Their rooms were on the top floor of a three-story building. As she leaned over the railing to look below, he had to remind himself not to hover. Cate was a grown woman. She was in no danger of falling.

"I'm glad you like it," he said. "I thought about booking a B and B, but I decided we might enjoy a little more privacy."

She looked over her shoulder at him. Her face was solemn, but her eyes danced. "Just to be clear, we're talking about sex, right?"

He felt his face heat. "*You're* the noisy one," he pointed out.

Her eyebrows went up. "Brody Stewart. That's not a polite comment."

"But factual."

When Cate laughed, something inside him relaxed. This was the place where he and Cate worked best. The intersection between carnal and casual. If they could keep their relationship easy and uncomplicated, this trip would be well worth the emotional and financial cost.

He shrugged out of his suit jacket, loosened his tie and unbuttoned the top buttons of his shirt. "I made dinner reservations for seven. Does that suit you? I thought we'd stay here in the hotel since it's our first night."

"Sounds perfect. I'll shower and change."

"You could still wear the dress," he said, hating to see it go.

Cate wrinkled her nose. "I'm rumpled and damp. I brought several new things. I won't embarrass you, Mr. Stewart." She handed him the strand of pearls. "Stash these in the safe, will you?"

He took the pearls and dropped them on a nearby table. "Come here, woman. I haven't kissed you in hours."

Dragging her close, he found her lips with his and dove in. The taste of her destroyed his good intentions. He'd intended to remind her that she was his now. What he discovered instead was that the ground beneath his feet was alarmingly unsteady.

Kissing Cate Everett, his lover, was one thing. Kissing Cate Stewart, his wife, was entirely another. Feelings he hadn't expected buffeted him from all sides. Tenderness. Protectiveness. Raw, urgent need.

He tamped down his lust with great effort. Cate leaned into him trustingly, her arms linked around his neck. "I'm too fair-skinned for many hours in the sun," she whispered. "I think we'll need to spend a lot of time in our suite."

"In bed," he muttered. It wasn't a question.

She wriggled closer. The slick fabric of her dress rubbed against his suit, creating some kind of erotic friction that threatened to incinerate him from the inside out. "Yes," she said, the word drawn out on a sigh.

In desperation, he thrust her away, holding her at arm's length until her eyes opened, and she stared at him. "I think we should pace ourselves," he said desperately. He wouldn't be accused of using sex to get his way.

Cate pouted dramatically. "I thought honeymooners usually slammed the door and went at it like rabbits."

"What would you know about it?" he asked, deliberately snarky to give himself time to ratchet down. "Have you ever been on a honeymoon before today?"

"No. Have you?"

"Hell, no. But I'm damned sure the groom is supposed to provide romance leading up to the main event."

"Romance isn't all it's cracked up to be," she said, her eyes reflecting memories he wanted to obliterate, memories of the idiot who had hurt her so badly.

He ran the back of his hand across her cheek. "Maybe you've been with the wrong person before," he said softly. "Could be that you and I are exactly the right combination, Mrs. Stewart."

"We aren't supposed to mention weddings and honeymoons and my new marital status," she reminded him.

"You started it," he said. "Go take your shower, Catie girl. I'll wait for you." He would wait forever if need be.

Fifteen

Cate stepped out of her unique wedding dress with more than a little wistfulness. Today, standing beside Brody Stewart and saying her wedding vows in front of a judge, she felt beautiful and desired. The fact that it was more sex with Brody than soul-mates-until-the-end-of-time was a distinction that didn't bother her at the moment.

She was in Key West with a sexy, ruggedly handsome man who wanted to make love to her nonstop for four days. That kind of thing was good for a woman's self-esteem. Particularly when she was growing out of all her clothes and already finding small silvery stretch marks.

The bath enclosure was decadent in the extreme—four separate showerheads and walls of beautiful taupe

marble veined in gold. She wrapped a towel around her
head to protect her hair and stepped in with a sigh of
pleasure. As she washed with the expensive shower gel
she found in the caddy, she got hot and shaky as she
thought about the hours to come.

Was it normal to feel so wanton, so out of control?
The thought of his hands caressing her breasts made
her knees wobbly.

When she was clean and dry, she tweaked her hair
and then rifled through her collection of brand-new
maternity clothes. At her recent doctor's appointment,
the scales had reflected an increase, but nothing too
terrible. Tonight was her wedding night. She wanted
to look extra special.

Fortunately, one dress fit the bill. Since joining a
couple of social media groups for expectant moms,
she had discovered all sorts of helpful advice. One de-
signer in particular was known for creating special-
occasion dresses that would expand along with a pregnant
woman's waistline.

Cate had researched and ordered a slender tank dress
made of ribbed cotton gauze that fell to her ankles.
Spaghetti straps braided from the same fabric were in-
tertwined with tiny gold metallic strands. The colors
were an impressionist canvas of celadon, ivory, tan-
gerine and gray.

The soft translucent fabric was lined with a similar
thin gauze in ecru. Though the dress clung from shoulders to knees, the style and the fabric were flattering
in the extreme.

After touching up her mascara and adding a bit of

eye shadow for evening drama, Cate stepped back and examined her reflection in the mirror. Her eyes danced with excitement. Maybe Brody was right. Once the baby came, it would be a very long time before Cate had the same freedom she enjoyed now. It made sense to enjoy this trip and her companion.

She tiptoed back into the living room, hoping to surprise him. Instead, she was the one to suck in a startled breath. Brody lay sprawled on the sofa deeply asleep. He had unbuttoned his shirt all the way, giving her a tantalizing glimpse of hard male abdomen.

The man was ridiculously ripped. All that boating, presumably.

She knelt beside him on the rug. The evidence of late-day stubble shadowed his jaw. His eyelashes were long and thick, his nose straight and masculine. If her baby was a boy, she wanted him to look like Brody.

Without warning, the truth washed over her, drowning her in a sea of dismay and giddy certainty. She was in love with Brody Stewart. Despite her Ivy League academic education and her twenty-first-century feminist sensibilities that might pooh-pooh the idea of love at first sight, she had met him last October and fallen head over heels almost the first instant.

Why else would she have broken her sexual dry spell in a way that was so unlike her usual behavior?

She sat there for minutes, maybe even an hour. Who knew? All she wanted to do was watch the steady rise and fall of his broad, sculpted chest. Even as she clung to the sweetness of the moment, she knew she would never have all of him. Knew it and accepted it. Just as she knew and accepted the fact that he would leave her and break her heart.

Brody was a man not easily tamed or housebroken. He wanted to do his duty by this baby, though that would not be a full-time job. Like her parents, he would provide for Cate's needs, but he would move on.

In those quiet moments, she made peace with her future. It hurt. The pain was a great jagged wound, ripping her in two. Even so, she said her prayers and accepted her fate. She had Brody for a time. That would have to be enough.

At last, he stirred, those movie-star lashes lifting slowly. "Sorry," he muttered. "I must have been more tired than I thought."

She managed a smile. "It's okay. I like watching you sleep."

His grin held only a fraction of its usual wattage. "Isn't that the man's line?"

Leaning forward, she kissed him softly. "I think we're inventing our own rules," she said.

He curled a hand behind her neck and held her close when she would have pulled away. "I like the dress," he muttered. "Can't wait to take it off you."

"Dinner first," she reminded him, trying not to let him see how completely undone she was. She would have to get a handle on her careening emotions, or he would know something was up.

She was strong. She could handle many difficult challenges and situations. But having Brody know she was in love with him was not one of them.

It was bad enough that he felt obligated by this tiny

unborn baby. Cate refused to be the poor, pitiful woman who pleaded for his love.

She stood up as gracefully as she could, given the circumstances, and held out a hand to help him to his feet. "The shower's all yours," she said lightly.

He nodded, though his gaze was keen as he looked her over. "You okay, Catie girl? Your cheeks are pink."

"I'm great. But if you wait much longer, I'm going down to dinner without you."

He held up his hands. "I'm going. I'm going."

Much later, Cate leaned her chin on her hand and yawned. "I ate way too much," she said.

On the other side of the linen-clad table, Brody took a sip of his wine and smiled. "It was a verra good meal," he drawled. He had changed into a fresh suit and tie, this one with a blue shirt that emphasized his eyes.

They had talked about innocuous subjects over dinner. Now she wanted more from him. "Tell me about the ocean," she said. "How did you end up loving boats?"

Brody's hand stilled midsip. He finished his drink and set the glass aside. Shrugging, he shot her a strange look. "Don't really know. My parents didn't own boats, but many of their friends did. I think I probably spent time out on the water with people we knew when I was very young. Loving the water goes as far back as I can remember...when I was only a wee lad."

"Wasn't that odd? For a child to be out on the water? Isn't it dangerous?"

"Not if you teach a bairn how to follow the rules. I

knew how to sail a small craft on my own by the time I was thirteen."

"I see."

"I don't know that you do, lass. Skye is a small place. Everybody knows everybody else. For teenagers, the isolation and lack of amenities can be suffocating. For me, getting out on the water was a means of escape. The world was bigger out there."

"And somehow your passion turned into a business?"

"Aye. Eventually. I went away to university in Edinburgh. Studied business. Came home to Skye and bought my first commercial fishing vessel. It was small and dirty and stank like rotten fish, but I turned a profit the second year. By then I was hooked, pardon the pun. I'd never been able to see myself as the kind of bloke who holed up in an office and wrangled numbers. Making a living from the sea is very satisfying, whether it be fishing or entertaining tourists."

"But you don't technically have to do the work yourself anymore, right? You've become successful."

He frowned slightly. "I could sit at home and count my money, if that's what you mean. Aye. They don't need me on a day-to-day basis. The various endeavors run fairly well without me. But a ship without a captain at the helm can wander off course. I have to make the major decisions."

"Makes sense…" Did he think she was lobbying for him to stay in the US? She would never do that, even if there was a chance he would agree. It was beyond clear that Brody Stewart was a Scotsman to the core, and one who needed home to flourish.

To be honest, she would have entertained the idea of moving to Scotland permanently for a man who loved her, heart and soul. But that man was not Brody, and he had never once even hinted at the idea of Cate relocating as a possibility.

With an inward sigh, she finished her last bite of key lime tart and tried not to think about how many calories it had. This was her honeymoon, damn it.

Brody summoned the waiter with their check. "We don't want to miss sunset," he said.

While Brody was in the shower earlier, Cate had read a pamphlet about the history and quirks of Key West. According to the travel guide, the locals hosted a sunset celebration every night of the year, weather permitting, at Mallory Square. From their suite, she and Brody could overlook the festivities, but he had suggested a walk after dinner. Cate had jumped at the chance.

Outside, the night was humid but not terribly hot like it would be later in the summer. Crowds had gathered all along the waterfront. Street performers of every kind plied their trades and posed for tips. Acrobats. Mimes. Musicians and artists. The atmosphere was something like Times Square on New Year's Eve but on a much smaller and more laid-back scale.

Brody tucked an arm around her waist. "Tell me when you want to go back," he said. He steered a lazy path through the crowds, careful to keep Cate from being crushed. Anytime she stopped to look at something, he smiled indulgently and stayed at her side. She couldn't resist buying a small, red, hand-painted Christmas ornament. The ball was dated for the current year.

Was it a good thing or a bad thing that Cate would have a reminder of this trip?

They paused momentarily when the excitement in the square picked up. The sun—a huge, red-gold orb—dropped low in the sky, kissed the horizon and sank into the ocean with a dramatic splash of color.

Hundreds of people clapped and cheered.

"I see why everyone celebrates," she said, leaning into Brody and soaking up the moment.

Brody nodded. "I'm partial to home, but even I have to admit the sunset here is spectacular." He kissed her temple. "A nice way to mark the day."

On the far side of the square they found themselves at the edge of the charming shopping district. The famous Duvall Street stretched for over a mile, filled with quirky shops and unique restaurants. Though the Keys had been hard hit by a recent hurricane, the area was rebounding slowly but surely. The locals were determined to reclaim paradise.

Brody tugged her to a halt. "I want to go in here," he said.

Cate glanced at the storefront. The elegant window display was filled with expensive jewelry. "Why?"

He rolled his eyes. "You're not that naive. I want to buy you a wedding gift. Something, in fact, that I should have given you before now."

"Oh, but I—"

Brody ignored her protest and steered her inside. The proprietor took one look at the tall, well-dressed Scotsman and beamed a greeting.

"How may I help you, sir? Ma'am?"

Brody lifted Cate's left hand. "We need an engagement ring. It was a fast wedding, and this bride deserves a stone as special as she is."

"No, Brody," Cate stuttered beneath her breath. A fake wedding didn't require jewelry.

He ignored her. "I'd like to see loose stones. Emeralds to match her eyes."

"Of course." The man reached beneath the counter and opened a safe. Muttering to himself, he sorted through several small packets until he found the one he wanted. "Here we go," he said triumphantly. He held out his hand, palm flat. The jewel he had selected was a deep, brilliant green. It caught the light and sparkled beautifully.

Brody picked up the emerald and examined it under the nearby microscope. "Very nice," he said.

Freaking understatement of the year. "Brody," she whispered. "I don't need something that expensive. I'm fine with the wedding ring you gave me."

He frowned at her. "Well, I'm not." He pinned the merchant with a sharp gaze. "Origin? Size?"

"Colombian. Three carats. As fine a stone as I've seen in the past twenty years."

"We'll want a setting to match the wedding ring. Something plain. I don't want to detract from the stone." He turned to Cate. "Do you like it, Catie girl? I can buy a diamond if you'd rather have that."

She gulped. "Um, no. No diamonds. The emerald is incredible. But seriously, Brody, I—"

He had already turned away and was examining the tray of platinum settings. A moment later he selected a traditional six-prong style that would cradle the emerald. The salesman scribbled something on a small slip of paper. He showed it to Brody. Brody nodded.

And it was done. Brody handed over his credit card.

The man practically danced with joy. "Give me an hour," he said. "And I'll have it ready for you."

Outside, Cate fretted. "I know that ring costs a fortune, Brody. You want to provide for the baby, and I appreciate your help. But I don't need an engagement ring, really I don't."

"Too late," he said blandly. "The deed is done."

"I'll give it back when the marriage is over."

For a brief moment she quailed at the fire in his eyes. Fury blazed. But he brought himself under control rapidly. "Ye're being rude, lass. It's a gift between lovers. We agreed not to discuss other topics, remember?"

He had his hands on her bare shoulders. Because of the press of people on the street, they were standing close, her rounded belly touching him. She stared into his eyes, trying to decide if she noted anything there other than male hunger. "I'm sorry," she said. "I'm not accustomed to having men give me extravagant presents."

His lips quirked in a wry smile. "This is verra new to me, as well, lass. Do ye want to go to the hotel while we wait for the ring?"

She took a chance and went up on her tiptoes to kiss him square on the mouth. The shock on his face was worth any momentary discomfort at being the first one to make a move. The man needn't think he was in charge all the time. "My doctor said walking is good for me. It's a perfect evening. I'm up for a leisurely stroll."

Brody blinked. "Well, okay, then. Let's walk."

For Cate, it was a night filled with magic. She might be a shotgun bride with a baby on the way, but romance was definitely in the air.

All along Duvall Street, humanity ebbed and flowed, bracketed with tropical flowers and steel drum melodies. Music spilled from bars and restaurants. Laughter and chatter filled the air.

Brody held her hand, his grip firm as if he was afraid she might disappear into the crowd. Cate shut her mind to the past and the future and concentrated on the present. No matter what happened down the road, she would have the memories of this night to sustain her.

At last, they turned around and made their way back to the jewelry store. The salesman—whom they discovered was actually the owner—was ready for them. He held up a small black-and-gold bag. "All set, Mr. Stewart. I've put it in one of our very best boxes. Though I'm guessing the lady would like to wear it."

His arch smile was too much for Cate. She hung back.

Brody took the bag. "I don't know about the lady, but *I* want to see the emerald on her finger."

He opened the box, removed the ring and then tucked the packaging into his inside coat pocket. Going down on one knee, he took both of Cate's hands in his. "I've mucked this up, Catie girl. But will you agree again to be my bride?" Without waiting for permission, he gently

pushed the ring onto the appropriate finger of her left
hand until it nestled against the wedding band.

"Oh, Brody."

The ring was exquisite, perhaps the most beautiful
piece of jewelry she had ever seen, much less owned.
His big thumb caressed her knuckles. "I can't get off
this damned hard floor until you give me an answer."

Cate laughed softly. "Aye, Mr. Stewart. I'll be your
bride."

At last, he stood and kissed her, apparently unconcerned they were being observed.

Cate's stomach fell to her knees and whooshed up-
ward again like the elevator at the Empire State Building. Too much excitement for one evening. She was
dizzy with happiness.

"Brody," she whispered. "Let's go back to our room."

His eyes darkened to navy. "I'm no' an experienced
groom, but I know a good offer when I hear one."

As they made their way to the hotel, all of Cate's
doubts returned a hundredfold. How could she make
love to him and still protect herself? How terrible was
it when one loved and the other did not?

Once Brody unlocked the door to their suite and they
stood in the elegant sitting room, everything became
awkward. They had already eaten and showered. There
was nothing left to do except for that thing newlyweds
enjoy on their wedding night.

Her heart was beating so fast and so hard she was
afraid she might get sick again or faint.

Brody was no fool. He cupped her face in warm

hands. "You're trembling, Catie girl. What's wrong? Talk to me."

"Nothing's wrong," she lied. "Not exactly. But I got married today, and things are different." *And I know now that I'm in love with you.*

He shook his head, folding her close against his chest and stroking her hair. "Not different at all, lass. We're the same two people. We want each other, and we're going to spend a long, wonderful night together. Nothing has changed, I swear. No need for nerves."

Brody was trying to comfort her, but every word he uttered underscored the bitter truth. For him, this was a marriage of convenience. For Cate, the mockery of what this relationship *ought to be* rubbed salt into a wound. Brody could brush aside the implications of the marriage license and the vows because they meant little to him. He wasn't in love with her.

But it was painfully different for Cate.

Sixteen

Brody knew something was wrong, but he hadn't a clue how to fix it. Cate was almost rigid in his embrace. Her distress was palpable. He played with her hair and murmured to her in Gaelic until at last her body relaxed. Only then did he scoop her up in his arms and carry her into the bedroom.

Though his instinct was to bend her over the lace-covered bed and take her wildly, he kept a tight leash on his hunger. Women put great stock in things like romantic wedding nights. He wouldn't ruin the moment for Cate.

He set her on her feet and played with the narrow straps at her shoulders. "Are ye wearing anything underneath this dress, Catie girl?"

Finally, a small smile tilted her lips. "Not much. Feel free to explore."

He sucked in a deep breath and exhaled slowly. The soft, gauzy fabric of Cate's outfit had neither buttons nor zippers. After a few moments of study, he deduced that all he had to do was peel it carefully over her body in order to remove it.

To keep himself in check, he started slowly. He tugged the straps down her arms to her elbows. The bodice bunched up just above the tips of her breasts. His hands were clammy. Very deliberately, he tugged again and sighed as she was bared to him from what once was her waist all the way up.

"I still can't get used to these curves," he said. He brushed her nipples with his thumbs and cupped the warm weight of her in his two hands.

Cate stood unmoving, her gaze downcast.

"Look at me, lass."

When she finally raised her head and her eyes met his, he realized with no little shock that his Cate was as aroused as he was. Her cat eyes sparkled, and her cheeks were flushed.

Experimentally, he rolled the tips of her breasts between his fingers and tugged. Cate's low groan went straight to his groin and hardened his erection to a painful degree.

"Don't move," he said raggedly.

He ripped his shirt from his pants and dragged at the buttons, popping loose at least two in the process. With his tie strangling him, he shrugged out of the shirt and finally managed to ditch the tie, as well.

Cate's eyes fastened on his chest. She laid a palm flat over the spot where his heart hammered wildly. "You're a beautiful man, Brody Stewart," she whispered, stroking him until he could barely breathe.

"You keep stealing my lines," he croaked. How far was it to the bed? He was losing control.

Cate touched his belt buckle. "May I?"

He couldn't have answered either way if his life depended on it. His throat closed up entirely.

Her small, deft hands dealt with button and zipper and fly. Soon, she grasped him and sighed.

Brody steeled himself. Letting Cate play when he wanted to rush headlong to the main event was virtually impossible. Her fingers squeezed and measured and stroked with careful reverence that destroyed him.

"Cate…" The single syllable was guttural.

She looked up at him. "Too much?" Her eyes were huge.

"Not enough."

He took the reins again and gently finished removing her dress. Now her only adornment was silver hoop earrings, strappy, high-heeled sandals and the rings he had placed on her finger.

Her ripe, lush body was incredibly beautiful and alluring—like a Gauguin he had once seen in the Louvre during a school trip. As a teenage boy, he had understood the lust of male for female, but not the deep, wrenching need to please a woman.

Feeling remarkably light-headed, he kicked off his shoes, removed his socks and stepped out of his trousers. His erection stood flat against his belly. Cate's eyes rounded slightly as if she had never seen him like this before.

Suddenly, he lost his nerve. This was Cate's wedding night. He'd told her it didn't matter, but he was wrong. It mattered a hell of a lot. He had given her his name and his ring, if not his heart. Tonight she deserved to be wooed and taken with every ounce of finesse he could muster.

He took one of her hands in his. "Come with me."

The bed was tall and covered in pillows. He tossed them all aside but two and folded back the fancy duvet. The sheets were crisp and cool to the touch. Again, he lifted her, intending to lay her on the mattress. But this time she was naked. The feel of her in his arms fried his brain.

He felt like a caveman faced with a glorious princess. "You're the most beautiful thing I've ever seen," he muttered. "When I first set eyes on you last October, I knew you were going to be trouble." He said it teasingly, but the truth of that statement resonated in his gut.

Something about Cate Everett made him a little insane.

Her hands were linked behind his neck. When she kicked her feet, both shoes went flying. "Are we going to talk all night?"

Her little pout forced a choked laugh from his parched throat. "God, I hope not."

He dropped her on the bed and chuckled when she bounced and protested. Then he was down beside her, his hands roving her body like a blind man learning the curves and valleys of a perilous journey.

Cate was larger now, and infinitely more lovely. He pressed his fingertips on either side of her navel and bowed his head when Baby Stewart kicked in protest. "Is the sex okay?" he asked. "Do we have to be careful?"

"No more careful than usual," she said.

Suddenly, he wanted her on top more than any other position he could think of. "How about this for starters?" He sprawled on his back and helped her move astride him.

She bit her lip, her expression anxious. "Are you sure, Brody? I must look like a cow from this angle."

He scowled. "Don't be absurd. I want you so badly I'm shaking, Cate. Do I seem like I'm repulsed by you?"

"Oh," she said, chastened. "Okay. I thought maybe you were just being nice."

He took her fingers and wrapped them around his rigid sex. "There's nothing nice about this, lass. I'm going to have ye now."

He grasped her hips and guided her down onto his erection. Her body took his eagerly, stretching to accommodate him, gloving him in warm, wet heat. *Holy hell.*

He closed his eyes and tried to breathe as he tried not to come inside her. Not yet. Damn, not yet.

Cate leaned forward, her hands on his chest. "Brody? Are you okay? Your face looks weird."

He started laughing and couldn't stop. Each time he laughed, her body slid another millimeter down onto him. "Ye're killin' me, Catie girl. I'm like a green lad with his first woman. I'm about to embarrass myself and you haven't even crossed the first gate yet."

His pregnant lover wriggled her hips and groaned. "I'm not as far behind as you think, stupid man. Do something. Move. *Please*."

For the first time it dawned on him that his beautiful Cate was as wildly reckless with lust as he was. "Aye." That was all he could manage. One short word. He thrust his hips and found the mouth of her womb with the head of his sex.

"Yes…" Cate was flushed all over, her face rosy-red. "More," she demanded. "More, Brody."

He lost it. All thoughts of rings and babies and wedding-night romance flew out the window. Passion consumed him, that and the need to make Cate irrevocably his. He worked her up and down on his erection wildly, knowing her pale hips would bear the mark of his hands.

"Cate. Ah, God, Cate." His climax slammed into him, rendering him rigid in release for what seemed like eons, and then lax with pleasure. With his last vestige of sanity, he found her pleasure spot and rubbed it.

She came apart and cried out his name.

He rolled to his side and cuddled her.

Cate floated in a haze of contentment, blinking blearily as she realized that the pinks and golds of dawn had sneaked into the room. She and Brody had only slept in snatches all night long. The man was voracious. Not that she was complaining.

With a smug smile, she turned her head and examined his now-familiar face. Her *husband* slept deeply, obviously worn out from his many hours of vigorous activity. Surely Brody felt *something* for her. He was so tender, so sweet. Even in the middle of the night when they were half-asleep, he played with her hair. She had lost most of the pins along the way.

Though it pained her to leave him, nature called. After a quick trip to the bathroom, she washed up, donned one of the fancy hotel robes and tried to do something about the disaster that was her hair. She found the few remaining pins, removed them and brushed out what was left of her bridal hairstyle.

Though it would be nice to spend all day in bed, it did seem a shame to miss seeing more of Key West. Maybe they could order room service and then head out...

When she returned to the bedroom, Brody was awake and staring at his phone. Something about the rigid set of his jaw told her he wasn't in quite as good a mood as she was. He was still nude, but he had wrapped a coverlet from the foot of the bed around his waist.

"Brody? What is it? What's wrong?"

He shot her a glance. "There's been an accident. In Scotland. One of our boats rammed another one in the Skye harbor. Multiple injuries. There may be fatalities."

She went to him and slid her arms around his from behind. "I am so sorry. Is there anything I can do?"

He shrugged free of her light embrace, crossed the room to get his suitcase and began dressing with jerky motions. "I have to get back."

Her jaw dropped. "To Scotland? But we're on our honeymoon. Can't Duncan handle things?"

Brody turned around and shot her an incredulous look. "We may be sued."

"Don't you have insurance?"

"Cate," he said forcefully. "You aren't listening. You don't understand. If victims start suing my company, I could lose everything. *Everything*."

Perhaps she hadn't understood the first time, but she did now. When Brody said the word *everything*, he clearly wasn't including Cate and the baby. The *everything* he was so passionate about was all back in Scotland. His wife and his child were no more than inconvenient incidentals.

From the beginning she had known that loving Brody and losing him was going to hurt. She just hadn't expected it to end so soon.

The next hours passed in a haze of frustration and incredulity. Brody was on the phone constantly, wheeling and dealing and cajoling to change tickets and book new ones. By noon they had boarded a plane to Fort Lauderdale. When they landed, Brody quick-marched her to another terminal and another gate. He handed her a ticket. "I've booked you a first class seat to Asheville. And I arranged for a car to pick you up on the other end and take you to Candlewick." He paused. "I'm sorry about Key West, Cate. We'll go another time."

She hid every ounce of her hurt and despair. "Of course. When does *your* flight leave?"

He glanced at his watch. "Four hours. But it's from Miami. I'm renting a car. I'd better get over there."

"Yes. You should."

He took her by the shoulders and kissed her forehead. "Take care of yourself, Little Mama. I'll be in touch soon."

"Goodbye, Brody." She made herself walk away from him calmly, spine straight, eyes dry. This might well turn out to be the shortest marriage in the history of record books. When she entered the waiting area and found a seat, she waited a full ten seconds and then turned her head to look for him.

Brody was gone.

Seventeen

Brody had been running on autopilot ever since he received Duncan's text. Only by clamping down on his feelings and compartmentalizing every detail of the incredible night before was he able to function.

He had returned the rental car, checked in for his overseas flight and boarded the huge jumbo jet. Twelve hours later Brody tipped the driver and got out of the taxi. He'd spent a fortune today, and had nothing to show for it.

After landing in London, he'd taken a commuter jet to Glasgow. Now here he was, on Duncan's doorstep. Brody hadn't wanted to go to his own place, because the air would be hot and stale, and he had no food at home. His stomach curled with nausea. He wouldn't think about Cate. He couldn't.

Duncan opened the door almost immediately, his face reflecting shock. "What in the hell are you doing here? You're supposed to be on your honeymoon."

Brody shoved him aside, went into the house and collapsed onto the sofa. "Give me an update about the accident."

Duncan continued to stare at him in bemusement. "Definitely our fault. It was the new guy you hired four months ago. He and the wife had a falling out. She tossed him in the street. He had a few too many pints at the pub before going on board for his shift, and the rest is history."

"The victims?"

"Stable. Eleven in all. Three are children."

"Hell."

"Exactly." Duncan grimaced. "I can't believe you didn't trust me to handle this."

Brody blinked. "Of course I trust you. Implicitly."

"Then why are you here?" Duncan's dark eyes judged Brody and found him wanting.

"I've put everything I have into the business. My boats are an extension of me. They're who I am. Cate or no Cate, I had to be here. Not because I don't trust you, but because I..." Brody stopped, scrubbed his hands over his face. *Because being with Cate scared me shitless, and I seized on this disaster as a chance to put some distance between us.* He sucked in a ragged breath. "The point is, I'm here to help."

Duncan scowled as the landline began to ring. "There's nothing you can do at the moment."

He picked up the phone and after a few moments

of listening, his face sobered. He looked like someone had punched him in the belly. "Sure, Granny," he said. "Do you want to talk to Brody?" Her response was loud enough for Brody to hear the volume if not the actual words. Duncan held the phone away from his ear, wincing. After a few moments he seized a break in his grandmother's rant. "I'll tell him. Don't worry."

When Duncan hung up, Brody stood, swaying with exhaustion. "What is it?"

Duncan's expression held both sympathy and pity, enough to curl Brody's stomach. "Cate is in the hospital. She's had some heavy bleeding. The doctor says she may lose the baby."

Cate picked at a loose thread on the thin hospital blanket and tried not to think about Brody. He was gone. She was in this alone. Even if he came back for the birth, it meant nothing. And besides, there might be nothing to come back for. Tears she couldn't stem leaked down her face.

She'd sent Isobel home hours ago. This was day two of Cate's hospitalization. The old woman was too frail for a vigil. Now it was dark outside, and there was nothing to do but wait.

The stack of mail Brody's grandmother had brought was little more than a distraction, but Cate reached for the yellow envelope and extracted the single piece of cardstock to read it a second time. Her friends in Candlewick were throwing her a baby shower. They were indignant and perplexed that she didn't know the sex of the child, hence the yellow card. Sharma was spear-heading the party-planning.

In the midst of her fear and panic, Cate was touched and grateful that she actually *had* friends who cared. She had locked herself away emotionally for the past five years. It was a wonder she hadn't scared them all away.

A slight noise from the doorway brought her head up.

"Cate," Brody said. That was all. Just her name.

She shook her head, not entirely sure she wasn't dreaming. "You look like hell," she said flatly. She was dead inside. Nothing could penetrate the ice in her heart. She wasn't upset that Brody had abandoned their honeymoon for a business emergency. That would be petty and immature. No, what cut to the bone was the way he had made it so very clear that his damned boats were everything to him.

"So do you." He hadn't shaved since she last saw him. His face was gaunt with exhaustion. His hair stood on end.

"I thought you went back to Scotland." She knew he had. She had tracked his flight online.

"I did. I was there for all of forty-five minutes be-fore Granny called Duncan and I headed back for the airport."

She shrugged. "You shouldn't have bothered. That was foolish."

"How are you feeling?"

She shrugged again. "How do you think I feel? You broke my heart, Brody. I thought you and I were getting closer, but you cut and ran at the first sign of trouble. I thought I was part of your everything. Now I know I'm not. And on top of that, I may lose my baby. I love you, Brody. But it doesn't matter, because you made your choice. At least I didn't have to guess where you stand."

Her cold, cutting tone made him go pale beneath his tan. "They said you're bleeding."

"Off and on. Apparently, it's common. There's some danger, and they've given me meds. Now I wait and see."

"I love you, Cate."

Brody blurted it out, uncensored. He'd figured out the truth sometime during the middle of his second transatlantic voyage. Cate blinked but didn't seem particularly overjoyed. "Go back to Scotland, Brody."

"I can't leave you."

"Correction. You can and you did. *Everything* you cared about was in jeopardy, remember?"

It was worse than he thought. Hearing Cate quote his callous words back to him was agonizing. "My mother often called my father a thickheaded, stubborn male when I was growing up. Apparently, I'm more like him than I realized. I'm sorry, Cate. I didn't know."

"Didn't know what?" Her air of calm showed cracks. "Never mind," she said. "Get out." Each word was an icy command. "I don't want you here."

"Can you feel the baby?"

"I'm not discussing this with you. If I miscarry, we'll have the marriage annulled. That's all you need to know."

"It's my baby, too. For God's sake, Cate. Don't be absurd."

A nurse came hurrying in and scowled at him as Cate's monitor began to beep loudly. "You'll have to leave, sir. Visiting hours were over long ago. You're upsetting my patient." She checked Cate's blood pressure efficiently and frowned. "Don't make me say it again. You need to go."

"I'm her husband," Brody said desperately.

The woman raised an eyebrow. "You're Mr. Everett?"

"No," Brody stuttered. "I'm Brody *Stewart*."

"Well, this woman is registered as Cate Everett, so I'd suggest you leave before I call security."

Brody turned to the silent woman in the bed. "Tell her, Cate. Tell her who I am."

Cate stared at him impassively. Those vibrant green eyes were dull and lifeless. "You're nothing to me. Go away."

Brody staggered into the hall and slumped against the wall, eventually ending up on his butt with his head on his knees. God, he was tired. Never in his life had he felt such overwhelming fear. The black hole inside his chest was sucking away every shred of hope he'd managed to cling to for the past unbearable hours. The only day that came close to being this dreadful was the one when he had finally understood his parents were divorcing.

Even that hadn't been as bad, because he'd had Duncan and Grandda and Granny. Tonight he had no one.

Why had he been so slow to realize the truth? Cate was his everything, not some stupid boat. At a deep, barely conscious level, he had been dealing with that realization for months. The truth had been terrifying, so he had stayed away from North Carolina. How could he have been so stupid? His deliberate, obtuse refusal to recognize the wonder that was right beneath his nose had ruined everything. He had let fear consume him. Fear of pain and loss.

And now the damage was done. All he could do was pray for answers. He had to figure out a way to fix this. He had to... Failure was not an option.

Fortunately, the night shift was sparsely populated. Nurses and aides walked around him gingerly, but no one actually tried to boot him out. At last, his body shut down. With his throat thick with tears, he slept.

Why did doctors have to do their rounds so damned early? Cate had finally managed a good stretch of rest somewhere after 5 a.m., and now, barely two hours later, her ob-gyn awakened her.

"Let's take a look," the perky, too-cute-for-school doctor said. The woman's hands were gentle as she folded back the sheet and lifted Cate's hospital-issue gown. She pursed her lips and probed delicately. At last, she lifted her head. "Breathe, honey, before you black out."

Cate hadn't even realized she was holding her breath. "Oh, sorry. Well, how am I?"

The doctor smiled. "As far as I can tell, the bleeding has stopped completely." She held her stethoscope to Cate's belly and listened. "That little one is dancing around in there. I think you're in the clear. But we'll keep you until tomorrow morning just to be on the safe side."

"Thank you, Doctor."

The woman left, and Cate burst into tears, noisy, ugly sobs that made her chest hurt. The relief was overwhelming.

Suddenly, someone sat on the side of her bed and took her hands. "I'm so sorry, Catie girl. So damned sorry. Please don't cry. It's killing me."

She sucked in a deep breath and wiped her face with the sheet. Brody's presence befuddled her. "I told you to go. How did you get back so early?"

"I slept on the floor outside your door. I saw the doctor leave. I heard you crying. I'm sorry, Cate." He pulled her close, his big, strong arms wrapping around her and holding her tight.

"You smell like stale French fries," she said, sniffing and still crying a little bit.

"I've been wearing the same clothes for three days. It's no wonder." He sat back and smoothed the hair from her face. "Are they sure?" His throat worked. "About the baby, I mean?"

Cate felt as if she were having an out of body experience. "The baby is fine. He's fine. I was crying because I was so relieved and happy."

Brody went still. "He?" His eyes widened.

"I wanted to pray for our baby, and I needed to know if it was a him or a her, so I made the doctor tell me."

"A boy…"

Brody looked poleaxed.

Cate felt far too fragile to handle any more emotional drama. "I'm fine, too, Brody. Please go. I don't know why you stayed last night. They're keeping me one more day, but it's just a precaution."

"I love you."

She took a deep breath and exhaled. "We had a scare. It's over. Back to business as usual."

"No," he shouted, slamming his hand on the bed rail. She shrank back in the bed. "I don't understand."

He took her face in his hands and stared into her eyes. "I'm in love with you, Cate."

"No. You're not. You made your choice obvious when you left. You've had several shocks in a row. And you probably haven't had a good Scottish breakfast in days. You're off your game. But things will get better. Go or stay. I don't care."

He stood up and glowered at her. "I'm neither a Victorian maiden nor an elderly aunt. I'm completely clear-headed. And I love you."

"Go pickle a herring," she said, her heart racing. "I don't want to hear your fanciful tales."

"Where's the ring?" he snapped, his gaze zeroing in on her bare left hand.

"They don't let you have jewelry in the hospital. It's a hazard. But not to worry. I left it with Isobel. I'm sure you can sell it on eBay. Or do they even have eBay in Scotland?" She was babbling.

Brody put his hand over her mouth. "Shut up, Cate. And listen to me." His words were perfectly polite, but she sensed the steel behind them. "I love you. This isn't a game."

Cate was tired and overwrought and wearing nothing but an ugly hospital gown. And that wasn't even counting the fact that she was still supposed to be on her honeymoon. She shoved his hand away. "If you care for me even the tiniest bit, Brody Stewart, you will walk out of this room and leave me alone until I can go back to Candlewick. By then I might be willing to have a civil conversation with you. But I make no promises."

Brody's face darkened. She held all the cards. No man in his right mind was going to argue with a pregnant woman who almost lost her baby, particularly if that very same man was responsible for ruining her and his honeymoon.

"Okay," he said quietly. "If that's what you want."

She stuck out her chin. "It is," she said.

When Brody walked out the door, she burst into tears again, only this time she cried into her pillow so no one would hear. She didn't know if he was out in the hall again, and she didn't want to know.

Somehow she had to pull herself together and make plans, plans that didn't include Brody. The baby would be the focus of her time and attention and love. No matter how badly she wanted to believe in Brody's impassioned about face, she dared not risk being wrong about him again.

For the remainder of the day she divided her time between watching stupid programs on the TV and talking on the phone with Isobel. Brody's granny didn't mention her grandson, and neither did Cate.

At eight the following morning, Cate's doctor signed her dismissal papers. "No strenuous activity for a week," she said. "And no sex." The last instruction was said with a grin. "I've seen that brawny Scotsman out in the hall, but you tell him I said to keep it in his pants for a few more days."

"Doctor Snyder!" Cate muttered, utterly mortified.

The other woman just chuckled and opened the door. "You can come in now."

Brody entered the room looking only a shade better than he did the last time she had seen him. When she cocked her head and gave him the evil eye, he held up his hands. "Granny said I had to come take you home." He held up a bag. "I brought clean clothes." He sat on her bed. Again.

Cate snatched the leather tote out of his hands. "Go back in the hall while I get dressed."

"I've seen you naked," he reminded her.

The gentle teasing weakened her defenses. He was being so darned sweet and gentle. How was she supposed to resist him? Tears welled in her eyes. Brody, his expression strained, held her as she cried. "Sorry, lass."

This time the storm didn't last as long. Cate gathered herself together and sniffed. "Stupid hormones. Give me fifteen minutes to get ready, and we'll go."

He bent his head, looking searchingly into her eyes. "Are you really okay? And the baby, too?"

She nodded, unable to meet his gaze. "We're both fine."

Brody stood. "That's good." He shifted from one foot to the other. "Should I call a nurse? Do ye need help with your clothes?"

"I don't need anything. Go, please."

The near-tragedy had left her shaky and emotional,

and on top of that, she had to figure out what to do about
Brody. Could she risk a marriage that wasn't emotionally equal? She adored the man. Now, seeing his reactions to this latest scare, she did believe he cared about
her and the baby. But love? His declaration was sus-
pect at best. He was feeling guilty on several counts.
She didn't want a convenient marriage. Eventually, if
Brody didn't love her the way she loved him, the entire
thing would unravel. The best thing she could do was
absolve him and send him back to Scotland.

Eighteen

Brody was worried about Cate. She was pale and quiet, too quiet. No conversational gambit he tried succeeded in coaxing her out of her silence. At last, he gave up. Pushing her would only upset her. He had done enough of that already.

Without asking, he had decided to choose the longer route home. Taking a section of the Blue Ridge Parkway would add only twenty minutes to their forty-five-minute trip. But it would also provide several opportunities to pull off and look at the view, thus getting Cate out of the car.

He was hoping like hell that something, anything, would help him break through her brittle shell. He loved her. Sooner or later he had to convince her that was true. And though it scared him, he had to offer her a way out.

One that wasn't what he wanted, but a choice to prove that he wasn't trying to control her life.

While she had made one last trip to the loo in preparation for leaving the hospital, he had read through the paperwork the doctor left with Cate. She was supposed to drink plenty of water, have regular mild exercise and not ride in a car or airplane for extended periods.

Now, after waiting for Cate to be wheeled out to the exit per hospital procedure, they were in the SUV he had bought for her, and the air was thick with tension. Seeing a turnout up ahead, he eased the car off the road. "Let's get out and stretch," he said.

Cate shot him a look but didn't say anything. They had barely been driving half an hour.

Unlike Key West, here in the mountains, the air was crisp and cool. He handed her a water bottle and watched as she drained half of it. "I brought some food," he said. "Granny thought you might be hungry before we got home."

His companion brightened visibly. "Anything to sit on?"

"A blanket. You want a picnic table or the hood of the car?"

"That picnic table is in the shade." She pointed. "But let's sit on top."

"Of course." Concrete benches weren't designed for pregnant women.

While Cate stood and stretched, he retrieved the basket of food and the blanket. He spread the blanket over the table and set out the containers. When he offered Cate his hand to step up onto the bench, she pretended she didn't see and hopped up on her own.

Granny and the cook between them had provided fresh roasted chicken, a fruit salad and homemade croissants. There was even an insulated carafe of iced tea. Brody would have preferred a beer, but the tea would do.

They ate in silence. Cate sat as far away from him as possible given the confines of the tabletop. She stared out into the distance where ridge after ridge of mountains stretched for miles.

Brody wiped his fingers and leaned back on his hands. "Are you in love with me, Cate?"

Her body jerked, but her answer was flat. "No."

He absorbed the hit, though it left him breathless. "Do you want to annul our marriage?"

The silence lasted for hours, it seemed. At last, she half turned to face him. "I'm not sure. I thought you wanted the baby to have your name. Legalities and all that."

"I did. I do. But I've hurt you too much. Like most everyone else in your life. So from now on, I only want what you want."

Her smile was wry. "So docile. So tame. You can't fool me, Brody Stewart. You would never let a woman call the shots."

"I'm sorry for everything, Cate. I know you don't believe me, but I love you."

For one brief instant he caught a glimpse of the pain in her beautiful green eyes. Knowing he was responsible for that distress turned the knife in his gut. His lovely Cate was hurting. Badly. And he was to blame.

She wrinkled her nose and swatted at a fly that had shown up uninvited to their picnic. "Here's the thing, Brody. I think you're right. You do belong in Scotland.

So it makes my life very difficult. I don't want to keep a father from his son."

"Then come back with me," he said, not even realizing the words were about to tumble from his lips. "Live there with me. Or in a separate house. The Scots love bookstores. We could make a good life."

Her lips trembled. "We've made such a mess of things, Brody. I don't know what to think anymore."

"We have to make decisions," he said. "You know I'm right."

Jamming her hands in the pockets of her lightweight jacket, she stared at him. "I see the guilt on your face. But none of this is your fault, at least no more than mine. You're wearing a hair shirt and trying to do penance, for what? I don't blame you for leaving Key West. I truly don't. Maybe at first, but not now."

"I never should have abandoned our honeymoon," he said.

"It wasn't real, was it? We both knew that."

"Cate, I—"

She held up a hand. "I need time." The words were dull. "Time to think this through. Maybe an annulment is the answer. Please take me home so I can see Isobel and let her know I'm okay. I don't want to keep her waiting anymore."

Brody tasted panic, but he was going to fight. "I'll give you what you ask," he said quietly, "but I won't stop loving you."

For an entire week Brody bided his time. Isobel, for once, had chosen to stay out of the middle of the mess Brody and Cate had created. She hovered over her young friend, clearly worried, but not offering advice. As for Cate, she read books, chatted with Brody's grandmother, spent time online creating a baby registry at Sharma's request and generally avoided speaking to Brody.

The three of them had meals together, but that was as far as it went. Brody slept in his original bedroom, Cate in hers.

Their marriage had lasted all of twenty-four hours.

At the end of the seventh day, Brody decided they couldn't wait any longer for a showdown. He had promised Cate time, but despite his best intentions, he was desperate. He had to win her over now, for both their sakes. Cate had to understand how he felt. It was critical for their happiness and for their future.

Decisions had to be made. Duncan was keeping him updated daily about the situation in Scotland, but Brody was far more worried about his bride, who seemed to be losing weight when she should be gaining.

Her face was thinner, her eyes underscored with shadows. Cate had been excited about her pregnancy. Now she drifted through the house like a listless ghost.

Tomorrow morning he would take her for a walk or a drive so they could have privacy, and he would lay his cards on the table.

He prowled the darkened hallways restlessly. Maybe he should have insisted on sleeping in the same bed. Now the gulf between them was so deep and so wide, he might never find a way across.

He had played the gentleman, trying to give Cate

space and time to heal emotionally and physically. But was that the right thing to do? He knew the incident had terrified her, because it had scared the hell out of him, too.

He had waited this long. Surely twelve more hours wouldn't kill him. Even so, he found himself standing outside her room like a lovesick swain.

Resting his forehead against her door, he tried not to think about the nights she had welcomed him eagerly into her bed. He ached to hold her, to bury his face in her hair and inhale the scent that was uniquely Cate's. She was strong and funny and smart and sexy.

How could he not have known he was in love with her? All those months in Scotland over the winter, he had been restless and grouchy. He'd written it off to the terrible weather and work stress.

The answer was so much simpler.

With a deep sigh, he straightened and prepared to walk away. And then he heard it. A small, muffled sound, but unmistakable. Cate was crying.

His gut twisted. His heart fell to his knees. Somehow, he had to fix this. Without waiting for an invitation, he opened the door. The room was familiar to him. Even in the dark, he found her. She was huddled beneath the covers.

"Cate," he said, sitting down on the edge of the mattress. He tugged back the covers. She'd had them pulled over her head. "It's me. Talk to me, Catie girl. I can't stand to hear you cry." She was wearing a soft T-shirt, tiny bikini panties and nothing else.

"What are you doing here, Brody? It's late."

Her voice was husky and raw. There was no welcome in her words. But she didn't throw him out immediately. He took heart from that.

"May I turn on the little lamp?" He needed to see her eyes, to gauge her reactions when he talked to her.

After a long silence, she sighed. "I suppose so."

The light from the low-wattage bulb was sufficient for him to tell that she had probably been crying for some time. Her hair was tousled, and her face was damp. He rubbed her cheek with his thumb. "I never meant to ruin your life. From the day I met you last October, your smile has haunted my dreams. I went home to Scotland for the winter, but somewhere deep inside, I regretted that decision every day. All I can tell you is that I didn't know what love was. How precious. How rare. You are everything I want, Catie girl."

"What about the boating business?"

There was no accusation in her question, but he flinched. "I can sell it if that's what we decide is best. Move here. Help with Granny."

"I saw how you reacted in Key West, Brody. You were beside yourself."

"Turns out, it wasn't the boating accident that freaked me out."

She frowned. "Of course it was. I saw you."

He shook his head slowly. "I was crazed and irrational, yes. But it was our wedding night that did it. I thought I had my whole life planned out so neatly, but after that night with you I was ready to chuck everything I had worked for. It terrified me. I've never felt for anyone the way I feel about you, Catie love. I'm sorry I handled things so badly."

"You couldn't get away from me fast enough."

He swallowed hard. "Aye. That's true. But when I arrived in Scotland, I came to my senses. It wasn't my finest moment. I ran away, lass, plain and simple. It shames me to my core. The only thing I can say in my defense is that our wedding night shook the foundations beneath my feet. It was incredible. I couldn't breathe for wanting you."

"And you thought that was a bad thing…" Her bottom lip trembled.

"Ah, hell, don't look at me like that. I've always prided myself on being in control of the world. When it comes to you, Cate Everett, I don't even know who I am. But I want to figure it out, and I want to do that with you at my side. You told me you don't love me. If that's true, I guess I deserve it. But if you were lying, I'd give everything I own for another chance to make you happy."

"My name is Cate *Stewart*," she said. She didn't smile when she said it, but she leaned into him and rested her forehead against his chest. "I've been so scared and tired and unsure of myself, Brody. I didn't know what love was, either. I'm worried I'll be a parent like *my* parents. I worry that I didn't know my professor was a cheating, lying scumbag. Then there's you. How do I know what I feel for you is real?"

His heart stopped. Nothing in the room moved. Not a whisper. Not a breath. He kissed her temple. "What *do* you feel for me, Catie girl?"

She pulled back and looked up at him with a wavering, lopsided smile. "I love you, Brody. Madly. Passionately. Like in the movies, only better. You protect me, but you don't smother me. You believe in me. You let me know without making a big deal about it that you think I'll be a good mother." She paused. "And at the risk of sounding shallow, you're a beautiful, sexy man, and I love the way you whisper to me in Gaelic when we make love."

His mouth dried and his throat closed up. He had to try twice before he could speak. "Thank God." His hands trembled as he smoothed her hair. "*Mo chridhe. My heart. I swear I'll never leave you again. I can't. I couldn't.*"

"Then I've made up my mind."

Alarm skittered through his veins. "About what?"

"It doesn't make sense to move now. I'm too pregnant, and I want to stay with my doctor. But as soon as the baby is old enough to travel, I'm going back to Scotland with you. I want to see the water you love so well and the wild Highlands and the heritage that runs in my son's veins. We'll figure out some way to take care of Isobel. I want to go home with you, Brody. Your home will *be* my home."

He shuddered at the prospect of what he had almost lost. "Ach, my dear, wonderful Cate. Ye're so much more than I deserve."

She linked her arms around his neck and kissed him softly. "Neither of us planned on love, Brody. Somewhere, somehow, we found each other. Maybe the timing was off, and maybe we shouldn't be having a baby so soon. It doesn't matter. As long as I have you, I can handle anything."

"I love you, Catie girl."

"And I adore you, you big, opinionated, gorgeous Scotsman."

He smirked. "It was the accent, wasn't it? Gets 'em every time."

Cate was floating. Though her body was large with child, she felt as if she were light as a cloud or a feather. Happiness effervesced in her veins. "Make love to me, Brody," she whispered. "I've missed you."

He stiffened in her embrace. "We can't, my love. It's dangerous."

"It's been a week. I counted. I'm fine, Brody. Healthy as a horse. And we'll be gentle and easy. Please."

The man was torn. She could see that. But she wanted her husband, and she wasn't prepared to wait a minute longer. Fortunately, he was barely dressed. She ran her hands over his hard, bare chest, feeling the ripple of muscle and the delineation of bone and tendon.

Brody exhaled on a ragged sigh. His large frame was rigid as if he was exercising mighty control. "You'll tell me the moment anything hurts you?"

"Of course." Sliding her hands around his waist, she eased inside his elastic-waist sleep pants and raked his taut buttocks with her fingernails. "It was a great wedding night. Now I want to see what you can do with ho-hum sex."

He reared back and stared at her, his blue-eyed gaze

sharp and mildly offended. "Ho-hum? I'm no' familiar with that one, but I think I've been insulted."

She nipped his earlobe with sharp teeth. "Sex can't always be like it was in Key West. I'm sure we'll lose our edge eventually."

"Woman," he growled, his tone terse with determination, "ye'd better shut yer mouth before I have to put you over my knee. I'll never get tired of making you mine. So ye'd best get used to it."

Before she could do more than gasp in shock, he ripped off her nightclothes and his own and thrust her down on her back spread-eagled on the bed. He gripped her wrists in two big hands, pinning them to the sheets. Then he stroked her pregnant belly with his erection.

She panted as her nipples pebbled and her skin tightened with gooseflesh. "I want you, Brody." She was desperate. It had been a long, miserable week. "Don't make me wait."

His jaw was clenched, his smile tight with arousal. "Waiting is good for the soul, Little Mama." He bent and suckled one breast. Her body arched and tightened in longing.

He smelled like warm, aroused male. The look in his eyes, even more than words, told her that he loved her. The brilliant blue was alight with happiness and something far deeper.

"I love you, Brody." Her throat was thick with tears. She had almost lost everything. Her baby. Her lover.

He bent and kissed her softly, careful not to crush

her. "No more tears, sweet bride. We're together now. You, me and our son."

With gentle hands, he rolled her to her side and entered her from behind, spooning her in an erotic position that left his hands free to play with her sensitive breasts. She moaned when he cupped them and squeezed them together.

"Oh, yes," she whispered, already near the peak after long days of wanting him.

He nuzzled the back of her neck, his breath warm on her skin. "When I'm inside you," he muttered, "I don't want it to end."

He was large and filled her irrevocably from this angle. Her role was more passive. She sensed that even now, he was trying to protect her. She moved restlessly, so close to shattering that her body strained for the peak. Grabbing his hand, she gripped it tightly. "Don't stop," she panted.

"Never," he swore as he thrust harder, faster. And then, he touched her where their bodies joined and made her fly...

Brody felt definitely strange, but it was the best damned feeling of his life. The woman he adored was in his arms, and they were both trying to breathe. "I think it's after three," he groaned. "Maybe we should sleep." At least one of them should show some sense. He was going to be a father. He needed to practice making mature decisions.

Cate wrapped her fingers around his penis. "I'll bet we could try for another."

"Cate," he warned, halfheartedly slapping her hand away. "You need your rest."

"What I *need*," she said, flopping onto her back, "is calories. I'm starving."

"Now that you mention it, so am I. I hope Granny has eggs in the fridge."

"And toast with butter and jam?"

He rolled to his feet and helped her out of bed. "Anything the little mama wants."

"Wow," Cate said, laughing. "I guess there are perks to this pregnancy gig, after all."

He slapped her on the butt and rescued her underwear and shirt. But then on second thought, he tossed them on the bed and caressed her rounded belly. "I have an idea."

"I hope it involves feeding me."

He perched on the edge of the bed and drew her closer. "Soon," he swore. His sex surged and flexed. "I have an urge to sit you on my lap."

"Sounds kinky." She giggled.

"You can bet on it, Cate."

As he joined their bodies, his lover sighed and rested her head on his shoulder. "This is the real thing, isn't it?"

He gripped her bottom and pulled her in, taking her deeper. "Aye, Cate, it is. I love you, my dearest wife."

"And I love you, Brody."

"Until death do us part?"

"Longer than that."

"That's all I needed to hear." And then he took them home.

Epilogue

Duncan Stewart strode into the hospital with his blood pumping and his stomach in a knot. The long-awaited moment was finally happening. Somewhere inside the walls of this vast medical facility, a tiny baby was being born, first in the next generation of Stewarts.

It was a great day, a glorious day. Brody and Cate, still newlyweds, were over the moon and wildly in love. Soon, they would be leaving North Carolina and going back to Scotland.

But not Granny. Stubborn, wonderful Granny Stewart was determined to stay in the home she had shared with her husband and to continue running the business they had built with their bare hands. No going back to Scotland for her.

Which meant that "someone" had to be sacrificed on the altar of familial responsibility.

Duncan felt the invisible noose tighten around his neck. He was single. He had nothing and no one to tie him down. It made perfect sense for him to be the one to stay with Granny Stewart and help her keep Stewart Properties afloat.

So what if Duncan was giving up his job and his home and his friends?

He was happy to do it. Isn't that what he had said to everyone who asked? His brother? His parents? His dear, ancient grandmother?

Everyone of them had praised his selflessness and his kind heart.

Duncan punched the elevator button, grim-faced, and stewed in his own deceit. He was a damned hypocrite. He was going to stay, of course he was. But only because there was no way out…

* * * * *

If you enjoyed this HIGHLAND HEROES *tale of
passion and family scandal, don't miss the*
MEN OF WOLFF MOUNTAIN *series
also from* USA TODAY *bestselling author
Janice Maynard!*

INTO HIS PRIVATE DOMAIN
A TOUCH OF PERSUASION
IMPOSSIBLE TO RESIST
THE MAID'S DAUGHTER
ALL GROWN UP
TAMING THE LONE WOLFF
A WOLFF AT HEART

***

*If you're on Twitter, tell us what you think of
Harlequin Desire!* #harlequindesire

COMING NEXT MONTH FROM

HARLEQUIN®
Desire

Available July 3, 2018

#2599 SECRET TWINS FOR THE TEXAN

Texas Cattleman's Club: The Impostor • by Karen Booth

Dani left town after the rancher broke her heart, but now she's back... with twin boys who look just like him! Given his secrets, he knows better than to fall in love, but their chemistry can't be denied. Will the truth destroy everything?

#2600 THE FORBIDDEN BROTHER

The McNeill Magnates • by Joanne Rock

Reclusive rancher Cody McNeill refuses to let photographer Jillian Ross onto his land, but then a chance encounter at a bar leads to an explosive night. Now he can't let her go—even after he learns that she meant to seduce his twin brother!

#2601 THE RANCHER'S HEIR

Billionaires and Babies • by Sara Orwig

Wealthy rancher Noah Grant has returned to Texas to fulfill a promise, but what he finds is the woman he once loved hiding the baby he's never known. Can he and Camilla overcome what tore them apart and find a way to forever?

#2602 HIS ENEMY'S DAUGHTER

First Family of Rodeo • by Sarah M. Anderson

Pete Wellington's father lost the family rodeo business in a poker game years ago. The owner's beautiful daughter, Chloe, holds the reins now, so it's time to go undercover and steal it back! But what happens if the sexy businesswoman steals his heart instead?

#2603 FRIENDSHIP ON FIRE

Love in Boston • by Joss Wood

Jules wrote off her former best friend when he left years ago. Now he's back...and demanding she pretend to be his fiancée to protect his business! She agrees to help, but that's only because she wants to take it from fake to forever...

#2604 ON TEMPORARY TERMS

Highland Heroes • by Janice Maynard

Lawyer Abby Hartman is falling hard for wealthy Scotsman Duncan Stewart, but when she learns his present is tied to a secret from her past, can she prove her innocence and convince him what they share is real?

YOU CAN FIND MORE INFORMATION ON UPCOMING HARLEQUIN® TITLES,
FREE EXCERPTS AND MORE AT WWW.HARLEQUIN.COM.

HDCNM0618

Get 4 FREE REWARDS!

We'll send you 2 FREE Books plus 2 FREE Mystery Gifts.

Harlequin® Desire books feature heroes who have it all: wealth, status, incredible good looks... everything but the right woman.

FREE
Value Over
$20

YES! Please send me 2 FREE Harlequin® Desire novels and my 2 FREE gifts (gifts are worth about $10 retail). After receiving them, if I don't wish to receive any more books, I can return the shipping statement marked "cancel." If I don't cancel, I will receive 6 brand-new novels every month and be billed just $4.55 per book in the U.S. or $5.24 per book in Canada. That's a savings of at least 13% off the cover price! It's quite a bargain! Shipping and handling is just 50¢ per book in the U.S. and 75¢ per book in Canada*. I understand that accepting the 2 free books and gifts places me under no obligation to buy anything. I can always return a shipment and cancel at any time. The free books and gifts are mine to keep no matter what I decide.

225/326 HDN GMYU

Name (please print)

Address   Apt. #

City   State/Province   Zip/Postal Code

> Mail to the **Reader Service:**
> **IN U.S.A.:** P.O. Box 1341, Buffalo, NY 14240-8531
> **IN CANADA:** P.O. Box 603, Fort Erie, Ontario L2A 5X3

Want to try two free books from another series? Call 1-800-873-8635 or visit www.ReaderService.com.

*Terms and prices subject to change without notice. Prices do not include applicable taxes. Sales tax applicable in N.Y. Canadian residents will be charged applicable taxes. Offer not valid in Quebec. This offer is limited to one order per household. Books received may not be as shown. Not valid for current subscribers to Harlequin Desire books. All orders subject to approval. Credit or debit balances in a customer's account(s) may be offset by any other outstanding balance owed by or to the customer. Please allow 4 to 6 weeks for delivery. Offer available while quantities last.

Your Privacy—The Reader Service is committed to protecting your privacy. Our Privacy Policy is available online at www.ReaderService.com or upon request from the Reader Service. We make a portion of our mailing list available to reputable third parties that offer products we believe may interest you. If you prefer that we not exchange your name with third parties, or if you wish to clarify or modify your communication preferences, please visit us at www.ReaderService.com/consumerschoice or write to us at Reader Service Preference Service, P.O. Box 9062, Buffalo, NY 14240-9062. Include your complete name and address.

HD18

SPECIAL EXCERPT FROM

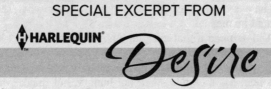

Reclusive rancher Cody McNeill refuses to let
photographer Jillian Ross onto his land, but then a
chance encounter at a bar leads to an explosive night.
Now he can't let her go—even after he learns that she
meant to seduce his twin brother!

Read on for a sneak peek of
THE FORBIDDEN BROTHER by Joanne Rock,
part of her McNEILL MAGNATES series!

Cody McNeill knew—instantly—that the lovely redhead
seated in the booth across the way had mistaken him for
his twin.

His whole life, he'd witnessed women stare at Carson in
just that manner—like he was the answer to all their fantasies.
It was strange, really, since he and Carson were supposedly
identical. To people who knew them, they couldn't be more
different. Even strangers could usually tell at a glance that
Carson was the charmer and Cody was...not.

But somehow the redhead hadn't quite figured it out yet.

Between the dark mood hovering over Cody and the
realization that he wouldn't mind stealing away one of his
brother's admirers, he did something he hadn't done since
he was a schoolkid.

He pretended to be his twin.

"Would you like some tips on what's edible around
here?" He tested out the words with a smile.

"Edible?"

"On the menu," he clarified. "There are some good
options if you'd like input."

HDEXP0618

The way she blushed, he had to wonder what she'd thought he meant.

And damned if that intriguing notion didn't distract him from his dark mood.

"I, um…" She bit her lip uncertainly before seeming to collect her thoughts. "I'm not hungry, but thank you. I actually followed you in here to speak to you."

Ah, hell. He wasn't ready to end the game that had taken a turn for the interesting. But it was one thing to ride the wave of the woman's mistaken assumption. It was another to lie, and Cody's ethics weren't going to allow him to sink that low.

The smile his brother normally wore slid from Cody's face. Disappointment cooled the heat in his veins.

The music in the bar switched to a slow tempo that gave him an idea for putting off a conversation he didn't care to have.

"Are you sure you want to talk?" Shoving himself to his feet, he extended a hand to her. "We could dance instead."

He stared down into those green-gold eyes, willing her to say yes. But then, surprise of all surprises, the sweetest smile curved her lips, transforming her face from pretty to…

Wow.

"That sounds great," she agreed with a breathless laugh. "Thank you."

Sliding her cool fingers into his palm, she rose and let him lead her to the dance floor.

Don't miss
THE FORBIDDEN BROTHER by Joanne Rock,
*part of her **McNEILL MAGNATES** series!*

Available July 2018 wherever
Harlequin® Desire books and ebooks are sold.

www.Harlequin.com

Copyright © 2018 by Joanne Rock

HDEXP0618

Want to give in to temptation with
steamy tales of irresistible desire?

Check out **Harlequin® Presents®,
Harlequin® Desire** and
Harlequin® Kimani™ Romance books!

New books available every month!

CONNECT WITH US AT:

Harlequin.com/Community

 Facebook.com/HarlequinBooks

Twitter.com/HarlequinBooks

Instagram.com/HarlequinBooks

Pinterest.com/HarlequinBooks

ReaderService.com

**ROMANCE WHEN
YOU NEED IT**

PGENRE2017

LOVE
Harlequin
romance?

Join our Harlequin community to share your thoughts and connect with other romance readers!

Be the first to find out about promotions, news, and exclusive content!

Sign up for the Harlequin e-newsletter and download a free book from any series at

www.TryHarlequin.com

CONNECT WITH US AT:

Harlequin.com/Community

 Facebook.com/HarlequinBooks

Twitter.com/HarlequinBooks

Instagram.com/HarlequinBooks

Pinterest.com/HarlequinBooks

ReaderService.com

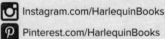 **HARLEQUIN**®

**ROMANCE WHEN
YOU NEED IT**

HSOCIAL2017